Have You Ever Heard a Butterfly Cry?

Lisa V. Taitt-Stevenson

Cover designed by AviLuxe Designs

Lisa V. Tait-Stevenson
Visit my website at www.lisavtaittstevenson.org

Printed in the United States of America

First Printing: April 2021
The Scribe Tribe Publishing Group

THE SCRIBE TRIBE
PUBLISHING GROUP

ISBN- 978-1-7362882-3-8 (print)
IBSN- 978-1-7362882-4-5 (electronic)

I would like to honor everyone that reads, purchases, glances at, or mentions this book and shares this book. Your support is felt and appreciated.

All Glory goes to God.

I would like to thank my sister for helping me with this work, my husband for his patience and support, my children for their encouragement and my cheering squad that reassured me throughout this journey.

Contents

And So it Began...

"Ok chick, I'm ready," she said.

"Ok, where do you want to meet?"

"Sky Zone."

She was still unsure about this. I could tell. I could hear it in her voice. We've been friends/sisters for 20 years, so I knew it was hesitation I heard in her voice. But she's determined. She's always been determined. She is Shanice Anderson-Jones.

"I hope she's on time." I said that more to myself than anyone else.

******

It was the first time we were getting the kids together in a long time, at least 6 months. I needed today. I needed to do this. But sharing my story, being this bare, had me scared shitless. When I walked in, all I saw was a whole lot of screaming kids and parents who could use either more coffee or a strong cocktail. Either way, she wasn't there yet.

"Chick, where you at?" I said when she picked up the phone.

"I'm parking. I'll see you in five," she replied.

"Ok, cool beans."

Five minutes later, she strolled in with that straight face that most folks can't read, but we'd been friends so long that it was easy for me. I could tell that she was serious and meant business. She smiled as soon as she saw us, but I had no doubt that she knew it was the day that she was gonna hear some shit that I'd never shared. Seeing her face when she walked in, I knew that she knew why I asked her to be the one I would share my soul with. Crap, I was scared. She's my girl, my ace but I didn't want her to look at me differently by any stretch of the imagination. She wasn't one to

1

usually flinch but this time she might. I wouldn't know until I started talking, but I knew that Kim could hear anything I put out and it would never go beyond her.

When they walked up, I smiled my best smile because I didn't want her to see my fear and I legitimately missed my nephew.

"Hey Thomas!"

"Hey Aunt Chickie! Hey Isaiah, hey Xavier!"

I giggled. Thomas, Isaiah, and Xavier always greeted each other with smiles and excitement. The boys, ages varying only by a few years, chuckled at their enthusiasm to see each other.

"Let's get them signed in and get a seat," I suggested.

We found a small table near the area they would play in. The table was small enough for us to be able to hear one another but not so small that we would be sitting on top of each other. I liked it better that way. I had on my hat in case I needed to tilt my head in such a way where she couldn't read my eyes. She had on a hat as well which meant if she tilted a certain way, I wouldn't see any disdain she might have as to what I was about to tell her.

We sat down and I took a deep breath.

"You can do this!" The girl trapped inside of me was cheering me on. I was scared. There were four parts of me, each wanting to speak, each with a story to tell. The child, the teenager, the young woman, and the version that sat in front of her right now. The first three quietly said, "You can do this." The current version of me, the one that sat at the table said, "You ready chick?!"

******

I watched her take a breath before she asked if I was ready. How fitting that she had on black. A black hat and black shirt to be exact. She usually wears color, but today the only bright colors were her lips and her sneakers. When she asked if I was ready, all I could say was, "Yeah give me what you got."

"I look at people on Facebook and what they remember about their lives and I don't remember much of my life except for the shit storms, if you will. I was four years old up until I left my house at forty."

She paused there. I'm not sure if she paused because the pain was rushing back or if she paused to contemplate if she was doing the right thing by sharing her story. I couldn't tell because her baseball cap was shielding her true emotions. So, I did what I've been trained to do to make a person keep talking and get them comfortable enough to feel like it's just the two of us. I had to make sure she understood that her secret was safe with me. I leaned in just enough for her to know I was interested in everything she was going to say. She looked to her left and began again.

"I feel like I played being an adult up until I was forty. I don't remember my children. I don't remember raising Symone, much less the very early part of Isaiah and Xavier's life. It sucks...it sucks, and I battle the guilt of that, probably a little bit every day."

Tears formed in her eyes as she watched the boys play without a care in the world. The tears filled her eyes to the brim, but they didn't fall. They never do.

"I look at adults, and the adults I see are more adult than me. It's weird because I'm waiting to wake up and be a grown woman. I have moments where I feel grown..." She paused for a moment. "...And then so much shit will happen and I'm right back..." Her voice lowered.

"I'm right back."

She chuckled. "I don't know if I can do this. I know I'm a hell of a faker. I can fake being grown well, but on the inside I'm four. Yet God gave me three kids so He must know something I don't. Maybe He feels like because of all my mess I will protect them at all costs, but I feel like I failed that one too." She shrugged her shoulders.

I looked at her. Shanice Anderson-Jones who was once four-year-old Shanice Anderson. I looked at her and saw the four-year-old who fights the over 40-year-old. I looked at her and realized that while she was speaking to me, she was wearing a hat that said, "Queen." The world sees Queen, but she sees broken.

"I realize that when I was sitting in my basement and I was crying asking God for someone like me, I essentially wanted someone I could control. And that's what I got. Marcus allows me to control more than I should because he knows what I need to make this marriage work. He knows I need it for me to function and survive in this marriage. EVERY RELATIONSHIP I GET INTO I MANIPULATE."

She said that last sentence forcefully. Not loud at all, just with much force.

"Without control, I feel like I will lose all my power, that I become that four-year-old once again that has no voice, no say, no opinion, as if I don't matter...and I need to matter.

"The only relationship that I didn't have any control of almost broke me. By the time I saw the monster and I realized I had no control, I went back to the four-year-old. I did whatever he asked. Nothing was ever good enough, nothing the four-year old did was ever good enough, and that was my first marriage.

"I fight the four-year-old me. I claw, I cut, and I'm mean. I call it being real. I call it truth, but it's survival mode. I'm nasty out of necessity to survive. From forty until now, she is who I fight with and who I fight for. Those were the Jackson fights.

Jackson is her ex-boyfriend.

"He tried to control me, but I refused to ever let anyone take me there again. So, I was four and I was forty and I fought, internally and externally. So, when the forty-year-old fought someone, she was fighting for the forty-year-old and the four-year-old and it was downright vicious. Four was when it all started; eight was when the realization hit me. In between those years, I was in training. By the time I was eight, I was in practice—damn near a professional. Shit—"

She paused briefly again as she blankly stared off into the distance.

"At eight, I can remember intentionally enticing a grown man." She looked over at the boys again. Her eyes welled again and like before she refused to let one tear escape. She sniffled to keep them down. She smiled at the kids before us who were no longer babies. She smiled with love for them and a cover for her pain. She turned back to me and I could see both—the four-year-old girl and the middle-aged woman.

"I can finally walk into a room and feel like no man wants me, because for so long I would walk into a room and feel like *every* man wanted me.

They wanted me for their pleasure, and I was so used to the attention that I walked into the room with that energy. I would socialize and "work" the room from a space of knowing that these men wanted only one part of me. So, to now walk into a room and not be noticed because I no longer walk with that energy is different. Not being seen in that way is like a breath of fresh air, like a weight has been lifted. But as freeing as it is, it is also uncomfortable. So, now I'm in a weird space because I don't know what to offer them. What can I offer them? For so long I didn't know what I had to offer anyone besides my physical being. It's probably why I give so much of myself to life-coaching. It allows me to offer something more. It allows me to give the very essence of me spiritually, not sexually. I can offer wisdom from roads I shouldn't have traveled, hope from the faith I have in my own mustard seed, and love from a selfless, agape space. I think it's why I hope my book and posts are well received because now when someone says, 'I accept you,' sex isn't a requirement for that acceptance.

"I'm in a place where I want to be known, I want to be heard, but I don't want to be seen. I fear that if I'm seen, I'll be right back to being four and I'm so mad that he has that."

She paused again and took a breath. Then her voice became like steel and she continued.

"I don't know if I'll ever forgive him. I'll have to go to God with that one." She wiped a tear I couldn't see.

"Did I tell you I got pregnant at twenty? I got pregnant at twenty and I got pregnant at..."

She searched to remember.

"I know it was before I was twenty-five. I just don't know when. I got pregnant because we didn't use anything, and we didn't use anything because I didn't say anything. I didn't say anything because I never said anything at four. I remember one guy saying, 'No one ever let me stick it in without a condom before.' How screwed up is that?"

"Hey, Kim." It was the parent of one of Thomas' friends.

"Hey, Dock," I replied.

I looked over at Shanice. She was finished. Not finished for good, just for today. She wanted to say more but she seemed relieved at the distraction. She didn't have to keep going back to the memories she worked so hard at suppressing for so long. She could let the child and the woman within get some rest. She could form a truce with them until it was time to talk again.

I introduced them and told Dock where Thomas was so his son could join the kids. Dock sat down and continued to talk to us oblivious to the depth of the conversation we were having before he arrived. She went into pretend mode. Pretending we were just having a casual conversation. So, we all laughed about the kids. We chit chatted and laughed until the kids' session was up and when Dock and his son left, we turned to one another.

"I guess that was it for us," she said with a sarcastic chuckle.

"Yea. Once he kept going with the conversation, I figured he was staying at the table so he wouldn't be by himself."

"Girl! He's a nice guy, but he can talk!"

We both laughed. We laughed harder than we needed to because we had to release the pain that sat between us. I needed to release the pain I'd witnessed so I wouldn't leave enraged at the phantom I will never know that hurt a four-year-old. She needed to release the pain of her story. The parts she revealed, the parts she battled with, the four-year-old that was trying to reckon with the forty-year-old who is mad as fuck.

"Thanks sis," she whispered.

Just then our little heroes in the making walked over, all smiles. We couldn't help but smile back because with them we are reminded that there is always hope, there is always strength, and there is always love. As we walked to our cars, we made a date to talk more in a few days.

The Phone Chat

"You ready, chick?"

She always seemed so confident, so sure. It even came through when she texted. It had been a week since we started our conversation and she texted me to let me know she was ready to keep going. I never believe in pushing someone to release things before they're ready. We knew this one had to be on the phone though. Her schedule was just as hectic as mine. It was the month's end and even though she wasn't sure whether she would have her job by the end of the year, she still worked like the first day she was hired twenty years ago. Like I said, it was month's end, a busy time for her and with the trials I had going on, I preferred to hear her out on the phone.

******

I called her. I'd sent her a text a few minutes prior asking if she was ready. Hell, I wasn't really ready, but I had to get it out and if I waited on her to ask if I was ready it wouldn't happen. Not because she didn't want to, it's just not her style. She doesn't push—with people. So, I texted her, and when she said yes I called.

******

"Hey, chick."

"Hey, girlie."

At that moment she paused. Nothing dramatic, just long enough for me to realize she wasn't ready yet. I knew though, instinctively, that she

7

would still go for it. As scared as she was to bare all, she needed this off her chest. Maybe that's why it came out rushed in the beginning.

"I spoke with Mommy today to get the beginning. I was a preemie. She had me at six months in the middle of a snowstorm. I was 2 pounds, 4 ounces. It was so long ago that the hospital sent my mom a telegram to let her know when to come get me. Mommy didn't have a crib or bassinet for me, so she made a bed for me in a baby bathtub she had purchased. I spent a lot of time at daycare. I can remember sleeping on a cot at daycare and every time I woke up, my shoes would be gone, and I hated that. One day, the same kid that would take my shoes pushed me into a radiator and I got a gash in my head. I ended up having to get stitches. My hair still doesn't grow in that spot. We never went back to that daycare."

Silence.

She was contemplating what she would say next and how. I waited patiently, then in a quiet tone she said, "I ended up having to stay at a sitter's house whose name was Barbie. Barbie had a son who made me cry every time I saw him. I'm not sure why; I still wonder what brought on those tears. I don't try too hard to remember; perhaps it's better that I don't." The pace of her words were slow and deliberate.

Another pause. That time it was longer. It was like she was going back to a time that would have been better if it could stay in the past. At that moment I could see her clearly through her voice. I could see she'd gone to a place that very few knew about.

"I was born a preemie because he sat on my mother's stomach and beat her the day before." The way she said it was so matter of factly that it was almost icy.

"I loved him so much. My father. I remember the day he left. He came home and they were arguing about the rent probably and she made him leave. I blamed her, but she never badmouthed him. She never tainted my image of him. She took the blame."

******

Kim was silent. I knew she was taking it in so I spoke slowly so she could absorb all of what I was saying. I paused like a smoker does when they take a drag, only I don't smoke. I paused because I was also wrapping my head around everything I was saying. I was telling my story and trying to understand certain aspects at the same time, and I couldn't. I started again.

"I loved that man. I remember one day he picked me up from my mom's house. I didn't know where we were going, and I didn't care. I was with my dad and that was all that mattered. And to top it off, he took me to the bodega and bought me a honey bun and a quarter water. We ended up going to his friend's house where they were playing poker. I'd never even heard of poker and there weren't any kids there, but that didn't matter because I was with him. While he was playing and winning, he was all smiles. We shared laughs and hugs; I was in all my glory. But then he lost it all and it was as if I didn't exist. I offered him two dollars. It was all I had from the allowance I'd been saving. I brought it that day. The look he gave me was the most loving look I've ever received from him and it was the only time I would ever see it because deep down I know throughout the years he tolerated me. The one time I needed him. The one time I needed him to be that man, I told him I wanted to leave my husband and he deterred me. Even though he knew all that I told him my husband had done."

My voice began to crack, and I felt myself get warm as my eyes started to water. I sniffed back some of the emotions, but she heard it.

Damn...this shit hurts.

I continued.

"I really would love to have a moment where I sit on my dad's lap and he hugs me. Just one day where he really hugs me, loves me, like how I love my children. Like, why do I have to meet him where he is?! Why the fuck doesn't he call me?! The only time I do speak to him is when he needs something. People ask him how I am, and he says I don't know. He doesn't know because he doesn't call me. It's probably why I expect Marcus to do so much. I expect him to fill a shoe I know he can't fill. But I've never envied my friends and their dads. I just wanted mine. My stepfather is the one who came the closest to filling my dad's spot. His name was Richard. For him it didn't matter what I did or didn't do because he loved me anyway. He was that dude that did all the things I wanted my biological dad to do, which is why he was so close to me; He was it for me. He took me for an abortion when I got pregnant with no judgment. He walked that journey with me and then convinced me to tell my mom.

"After him, I never let anyone who was that close to my mom get that close to me again. It's like since I'm reserving a space for my dad, I can't trust another person. It's why I believe a dad in a girl's life is key. Because when dads are involved, guys don't even attempt certain things. If I had just one person...him. I just needed him to tell me not to walk down that aisle with my ex and I wouldn't have done it. But I needed one voice, one dad. When Richard and Mommy fell out, I didn't see him anymore. I tried looking for him, but I couldn't find him. It felt like even he abandoned me."

******

Silence.

She was done. I could tell. It didn't matter how this looked on paper. Whether she said a lot or a little because she'd emptied her heart and that's where the story comes from. Her life story, her truth was all wrapped up in her heart and we had only scratched the tip of the iceberg.

A New Day

"I'd like to start somewhere else today if you don't mind."

"Ok, so where do you want to go?" I asked.

She was silent for what seemed like longer than a few moments. The air felt heavy like a weighted blanket. I attributed the weight between us to what she was about to reveal. I heard her take in a deep breath, and when she exhaled her words emerged softly as though we were in a room full of people and she was revealing a secret.

"Someone asked me a question today. They asked me how I was able to leave my ex when I did, and I told her Marcus gave me what I needed to leave."

There was a brief pause where the only sound between us was breathing and then she started again.

"He had told me for ten years that no one else would want me. That no one else would love me, but Marcus loved me unconditionally. Marcus loved me with all my stuff. So, he gave me what I needed, because he made my ex's words a lie. Don't get me wrong; I always had my mom's support, but it wasn't the kind of support to help me do what I always knew was best for me. I remember times I would tell mommy what he would say, but she never told me to leave. Instead, she would simply say, 'Oh well, why don't you give him another chance? Men will be men, and sometimes people make mistakes.'

"I look back now and realize that although she thought she was being supportive of my marriage, she wasn't being supportive of me, which is what I needed. Those words felt like a knife in an open wound because I was dying inside. I was dying because no one saw me. She was like so many of the women I was around daily. Each week I was surrounded by women in women's groups that I was supposedly helping but I needed help. I just needed somebody to say something. Should I have said something? Should I have said I needed help? Probably.

"It was easy to recognize the look of pain on the face of others. As soon as I spotted it, I would ask, 'Are you ok?' Yet no one saw the pain on my face. Most times in life, we move asking others that question not really caring about the answer, but we should. We should care about really wanting to hear what they have to say. That pause could mean life or death."

******

She was talking more to herself today. As she kept going, I realized this was a release. She was sharing, sure. But it was more of a release. She was giving me her internal conversation. Her private thoughts. She was giving me her weight.

"I was lonely. It was the loneliest time of my life. I think that's why I hold my shit. Because none of my friends wanted to know. They were so wrapped up in their pain—trivial or not—that they didn't care to stop and look at mine. So, I kept it. In my mind, at a certain point, I felt like they didn't deserve to know my thoughts. They didn't deserve my secrets. One of my friends—you know her. She once said, 'You know you never tell me your stuff.' I thought to myself, *Bitch, you were in my living room and you didn't give a fuck then so now you're just being nosey.* Instead, I said something a lot nicer that I can't remember but I held my shit 'cause she didn't deserve to know it...they didn't deserve to know it. It sucks that someone will reach out and ask me if I'm good and if they don't get a reply, they never follow-up. It's like they say, 'Oh well I asked, good deed done.'

She began to sob lightly. I let her.

"And now you're sharing," I said.

"Now I'm sharing. I...I'm sharing. Now I'm intentionally sharing because that girl, you know her, she and I should have been close. All that time spent, and she didn't see it. She should've seen it. So now I'm sharing. I'm not sharing because it has anything to do with my growth. I'm sharing because I don't want any other woman to experience that kind of loneliness. No woman should be surrounded by friends and be lonely. It's like I was in the water and everyone held my head above the water just long enough so they could get what they needed and when they got it, they left in their boat and left me to drown. They didn't help me get into their boat. I watched them get in their boats and go to dry land and I was still in the water, treading, left to drown. So, if airing my shit means someone else never has to feel like that, then I air it..."

"That's the feeling that causes people to commit suicide."

"It is. It really is."

Pause.

"I had moments, but for me it was waves. Most times I felt like I was losing it. Like an ongoing battle inside. I felt like I always needed to throw up. I didn't, I just felt like I did. Times when I didn't feel like I needed to vomit, I had to find a way to breathe. I was truly a shit show of emotions—a real shit show inside. I understand how people just snap. Like there were days I wanted to hit people with my car and that rage scared me. It scared me because I always carried it, praying I could hold it inside because I didn't know what would happen if I released it."

Pause.

"But this helps...giving it to you definitely helps."

I began to hear what sounded like a tapping noise on the other end of the phone. On my end I heard the chirping sound of my dying work radio. Maybe the background noise was always present, but I was focused on what she was saying that I didn't even faintly hear it. Maybe it was because she paused that everything else was intensified like putting an exclamation point on the fact that we're alone in our spaces looking loneliness and rage in the face daily trying not to succumb to the black hole it presents to us.

"Are you typing," I asked.

"I'm actually working on some stuff while I'm talking to you."

She moved back into her safe space. The one that keeps her busy enough for the background noise of life to stay at bay. It's the space she rests in, so she doesn't have to feel all the emotions of past pain. It's the space so many people move in, so they don't go into that black hole knowing there is no way out once you go in.

"Ok." It's all I could say. It signified to her that I knew where she had moved mentally, and we could be over for the day.

"Ok. I'm good hon, we can pick another day to do more work," she said as the keyboard clacking took over where her words once stood.

And just like that, the day's conversation was done.

The Space in Between

"What's in your head in between our conversations? What are you thinking before you call? Before you decide, 'I'm ready to tell more.' There's a space and I want to know what's in that space?"

I asked that question carefully. I wasn't sure what to expect. I was hoping she would write everything down and I could just develop it. But she wanted to speak. She wanted to explain it so I could hear her, and she could hear herself.

"Sometimes I have to get it out. Like a bad meal. You know? Like I just have to throw it all up. It bubbles inside the same way your insides bubble before you vomit. Only I throw up pieces of my soul, my past, my present...hoping to get relief. I wait for our conversations. I look forward to them. They're safe. You have proven over the years to be my safe place."

She chuckled. Not a nervous laugh but the kind of laugh that happens when you see a situation differently. The kind of laugh that's reserved just for the person laughing. The one that makes a person who doesn't know you wonder what it is you find so interesting that makes you chuckle.

"All I have is me so if I unload on me it's just me and my shit. But when something bubbles up, to be able to give it to you is precious because I know it's going on paper. See, I'm not giving it to you to carry, and I don't have to take it back because it's on paper. Can you imagine a loop? Imagine an event that just keeps replaying and even if you talk it out, walk it out, cry it out, it's still there because there was nowhere to pass it to until now. Now it's not me unloading my shit on me. I don't have to replay the loop because it's on paper. It's with you but I don't carry the guilt of it staying with you."

She paused. I heard her take a deep breathe in, but I didn't hear her exhale. Times like those I wish I could hear her thoughts.

******

I couldn't see her, but I knew she was writing. I heard her pen moving across the paper. I was waiting for that question. I knew it was coming; I just didn't know how it would be phrased. I'm glad she asked because there is a space I sit in before every phone chat. There is a space where, although I'm ready to get it all out, I can't put it all out at once because I'm not all the way ready. It's one reason I asked her to help me. I knew she'd move at my pace. She'd know when to push and when to wait. She would probe but not in a way where the four-year-old girl and the middle-aged woman felt threatened. So, I give her more. I needed to understand this entire space as much as she did, so I breathed in.

My story, my life feels like a lion in a room that's resting and suddenly that lion is awakened and wants to get out. That feeling is big and ferocious like that lion in that room. It's as if the lion awakens and all it sees are the restrictions of the room and it must fight not to tear its way out. As I breathed out, the words to help her get a clear picture of that space tumbled out...

"Sometimes I have a conversation with myself about my decisions. *Why did I...* This is a judgment conversation. I set my life up to a measuring stick. The same stick I use for others, I use on myself in these conversations only they're usually a lot harsher. When you judge yourself it's hard to win that battle. It's part of my constant chatter. It's the four-year-old me who battles the forty-year-old. The kid who wants to tell it all against the woman who measures her secrets against a bar that is probably set too high."

I took another deep breath in.

"The four-year-old wins which is why I talk to you."

I exhaled. I let go.

34th Street BS

"Ok, chick I'm ready."

"Ok."

I heard typing in the background.

"Excuse me, bear with me one minute while I send out a quick message. I'm sorry, chick flick."

I am used to her multitasking; it's what she does best when she's working, but right now, I need her still. I need her present so she can give me those pieces of her that she kept hidden. As I paid closer attention, I began to really listen to her strike the keys on her keyboard. It's amazing what you can hear when there is no background noise. Each strike of the key came across hard. Like a vibration you would expect from someone typing extremely fast, only she wasn't typing with a quickness, she was typing with a heavy hand. A heavy hand I wasn't used to hearing. She was putting her emotions in her typing. She was avoiding me.

"Do you need me to call you back?" I asked. I expected her to say yes. I almost hoped she did so she could gather her thoughts. She caught me off guard when she sighed and jumped right in.

"I was going to talk to you about this time he and I were in the car. Symone was still little, and it was freezing. We were in New York and it was close to Christmas. We pulled up to the 34th Street Station and he was looking for something in the car. I started looking around, trying to help him, although I had no idea what I was looking for. I reached into the backseat and grabbed a bag I hadn't seen before and a box of condoms fell out. I had never seen a box so big. I didn't even know they made a box that big. I grabbed the box and held it, waiting for him to explain but I knew instinctively what he would say. I looked at the train station and thought,

'Just leave, just run.' But then I thought, *'It's freezing, and Symone's not dressed right.'* There were all these people walking and smiling.

He got out of the car, probably to avoid the condom covered elephant in the car and I waited for him to return. As I stared out the window at all the people shopping for loved ones, holding hands, and sharing laughs, I couldn't help but think that I was in the midst of one of the happiest times of the year and all I wanted to do was run. I'd grown up taking those trains so hopping on one wasn't foreign to me, but I sat there. Frozen. Caged. Defeated."

******

She swallowed.

She then snorted a half chuckle before continuing.

"I didn't even realize he'd gotten back in the car. I just remember he said, 'It's not mine. I'm holding it for someone,' referring to the condoms I discovered. The person that he said he was holding it for was the person we came to 34th street to pick up, not to mention his wife was coming with us too. It's funny because he completely threw his friend under the bus with that lie. It was only when we saw that same friend that I knew that the lies would never stop.

"When his friend and his wife got in our car and settled in, he said, 'Hey man, remember that box of condoms you told me to hold for you?' You could tell his friend had no clue what he was talking about and in that moment, I knew he had no limits to the levels he was willing to go with the lies. He just didn't give a fuck about who his lies affected. It's crazy because his friend appeared completely caught off guard, but he didn't respond. What type of bullshit bro code was this?! I sat stunned. Not only was his wife right there, but his friend never said shit! I was speechless! I just couldn't believe that anyone would let someone lie on them in front of their spouse for the sake of bro code. I had a lot of moments like that. Moments when you know what you're hearing is a lie. Moments when you just want to leave. Those moments were a trip because I could see myself getting out; I could see me free of this relationship, but I was afraid I couldn't do it on my own, just like he said."

She paused. It wasn't long but it was long enough. The pause was long enough for me to know she was back in that space with him gasping for air, for hope. She was in a space I've seen with others far too often. That space where time knows no bounds and the past, present and future feel like one event instead of three. If I was in the room with her, I would have seen her eyes glaze over in the memory. I would have seen the tears that well up but never fall. If we were face to face, I would have had to relive the moment with her.

"Really Shanice, you can't just sit in the fucking car. You think you're a fucking princess."

I heard her sniffle back tears.

"And I'm like I just want air. Really? I just wanted air. I just couldn't understand why he would treat me like shit. God, I just wanted air.

"I was having a conversation with my mother shortly after this incident, and she stated, 'I know you've got a lot on your mind.' I thought to myself, *'If that shit in the car didn't break me, that day on 34th Street...if all I went through with that asshole didn't make me slit my throat, then I can get through anything 'cause he was another level.'* She didn't know the half. Hell, she still doesn't."

She paused.

We sat in silence until she was ready to begin again. The air was heavy because the story was heavy. She began as though she never made the comment about the memory of her mother. I didn't ask why either. It was one of those moments when a person has a memory inside of a memory, so I let her continue without interruption.

"We were supposed to be on our way to the supermarket when he said that. It was incredibly hot that day. He drove because I hadn't driven in years and didn't feel comfortable driving the truck, so he drove us everywhere. It must have been the hottest day of the year because as soon as I stepped outside, I began to sweat. That heat was serious! My daughter was still a baby, so he had her in the carrier. I walked over to the car and got in. I thought he was right behind me, but it wasn't until I got in the car that I realized he stopped to briefly speak to our neighbor. As the temperature rose inside the car, I opened the door to get some relief. All I wanted was some air. 'You think you're a fucking princess? Get your ass out the car.' It took everything in me to hold back the tears as I reached for the carrier my daughter was resting in. He gave me that look...the one that let me know I shouldn't even think about it. To make sure I knew his thoughts he said it. 'No, I'm taking her with me.' I walked back to our apartment that day with nothing. No daughter, no hope. The air I so desperately needed that day never seemed to come.

Sigh.

At that moment she paused, and I heard the sadness wash over her. I could hear it in her voice. The heaviness of hurt came through in her breathing. Then she said, "And I hate that he still looks at me, treats me like I'm still his wife. So, I avoid him. I just want to be in a place where I'm not his wife longer than I was his wife."

She chuckled to keep back the tears.

"In all this madness I had one moment where I had that possibility, that thought that it could work. It was when we joined the church. I mean we were going, and we were reading together, we were tithing, and he had excitement. So, I wonder now if he truly had a moment with God or was I just wishing, hoping. Like I thought I had him and then as quick as it came it left and I realized I never had him. It's amazing how you can be in a situation and wonder where God is, only to come out and realize He was always there keeping you."

I chuckled and so did she. It's a chuckle we often share when we understand each other's thoughts without words.

"Those two stories stayed with me all week. So, there you go, pumpkin. That's what I got."

Silence.

"So, what did you feel in those moments?" I asked.

"I felt afraid. I could see and taste freedom. I knew what my breath felt like free, but then my thoughts would begin to speak. *'Shanice you can't do it, you'll have to go back home to your mother.'* So, I stayed because I didn't think I could. But I never believed his lies. I always wanted to, but deep down I never did. So, every time I ate his plate of shit, I felt like shit. I felt like shit because I felt stuck. I felt like no one else would want me but it's a fucked-up feeling—"

Her voice started breaking.

"—to feel like no one wants you, not even the one you're with. My greatest hope was that he would tell me to get out, but he didn't. I guess in his mind, he had it made."

At that point she began to cry. She cried tears from that place. That darkness. Tears from the woman who just wanted air. Tears from the woman who just wanted out. I let the tears come and didn't interrupt because each tear gave her air. Each tear gave her that breath of freedom she tasted all those years ago.

"I hated that I couldn't be me, I couldn't be who I was when I was with him because I was always measuring myself against the chicks he was cheating on me with. Only that's not who he wanted me to be; he only wanted them to be those things. That's a mind fuck for you. Competing with what you think he wants. If they were loud, I was loud. If they were thin, I was thin. Only he didn't want me to be them."

Pause.

"Now I find myself battling to not do to Marcus what my ex did to me. I struggle not to now become the bully. Sometimes I laugh and think maybe this is God's way of saying this is me making up for the two or three nights I fell asleep on you crying.

She snickered again with tears.

"I don't know," she spoke softly. "The day he snatched me up by my neck I snapped at Symone, 'Damn, I'll get it for you, you just have to wait.' My response was simply because I was tired. But he snatched me by my neck and threw me against the wall and said, 'Don't ever talk to her like that again.' The crazy part is that he talked to me ten times worse. I was tired that day when I said that to her. I wasn't angry with her, and I didn't say it angrily; I was just tired, and she wanted what she wanted right then. That day he didn't want me talking to his daughter that way...but I'm someone's daughter too!"

Silence.

She was done. I could tell. She didn't say she was; I just knew. I could hear the tears. I could feel her pain. That was a place she never thought she would have to relive. It was a space she'd forgotten existed until the sting of her past felt more like the present. It was that space where her past, present and future blended into a space that defied its natural order. It was the space she didn't allow anyone in...until now.

Here We Go

"Ok...what we gon' talk about today! You ready?!"

I could hear the anxiousness in her voice. She was ready. More than ready.

"Yeah..." I replied.

"I was talking to Symone today and I was telling her my story, parts of the train station I shared with you. I told her so she wouldn't be shell shocked when she read it in print. I also needed to give her a why, but it's hard to explain what I'm just starting to understand myself. It's hard to explain all the feelings that were trapped inside me for so long. How do I get her to see that in that instance, as I was watching people go to and from that station that day that I felt like somebody unlocked the jail cell I was in and opened the door. There I tasted it—freedom—and then I said, 'Nope. Lock it back.'

"I was mad at God for not giving me the strength to leave."

Her breath stood still. I couldn't hear her breathe in or out. It was like there was air one moment and then nothing at all, so I waited for her to continue.

"I don't know when the crossover happened, and I stopped crying about me. Like I made more money than him, so I would've been ok."

She sniffled in an attempt to hold back tears.

"I didn't protect my babies."

That last line came out as a whisper. Low enough to barely hear, but a strong enough statement so it was clear. One of the saddest whispers I ever heard because it was mixed with both sorrow and regret. I imagined that at that moment she let a single tear fall as she contemplated the full effect of her not leaving and the trajectory her babies' lives took because of it.

"When you sit in shit and have kids you don't sit in it alone, and I carry all that guilt because I didn't protect Symone, Isaiah or Xavier. At the end of the day, our children expect us to protect them at all costs and I didn't. Each morning I get up and put on my stuff and put on that one uncomfortable piece of me I wear like clothing, and that's my guilt. I walk with it every fucking day. At this point I don't feel I deserve to be rid of it."

"So, you choose to put it on?" I inquired.

"Uh-huh, most definitely," she replied.

"Why do you feel like you have to hold it?" I was curious. Curious as to why anyone would still wear their guilt so many years later. Curious as to why she would continue to beat herself up when she spoke so confidently about loving yourself.

"Umm...because I see what he's done to her. How it affects her. So, because she carries that, I must carry this. If she walks in insecurity and not feeling good enough, I will carry this."

Her voice dropped and she began to sniffle again. She tried even harder to control the tears that wanted to fall. The tears she decided years ago she would keep locked in a jail cell with her.

"This is the shitty part of me I've dressed up to make pretty so no one knows. This is my secret."

I listened to her sniff back the tears, sniff back the hurt and the pain that sat in that deep crevice of her heart that she showed no one. That part that trusted no one, yet it held the hurt of others. One of them being her very own daughter.

"Saying anything more after that doesn't feel right. Complaining about some shit after this just doesn't feel right."

She paused, and then with the strength I've come to know, her voice changed, and she said, "It's amazing what we can do to hide some shit. I've said what I need to, and I will find another bag to put this shit in and take it with me. And we'll talk tomorrow like it was never said and we'll pick up where we left off.

"I've spent my life with all the stuff in my journey that writing this means the chapter will be done. I will get to write another chapter, but it will be new. It's like walking into a new house and getting to decorate. Up until now, I put blame on everyone else but after we're done with this project, I get to blame no one for what I write in my new chapter. I am running towards that new beginning, but I'm scared shitless, chick. So, I push, and I do it afraid because the one thing I'm sure of is I don't want this shit anymore. It's like when I put on my glasses, everything is clear— crystal clear. Here's the thing though: the new glasses make everything clear, but sometimes I don't want to wear them because I'm used to the blurred vision. That blurred vision is my comfort, and although I'm running to the next chapter, the new glasses scare me, and I don't want to be afraid to put these new glasses on."

She said it with a half laugh but the nervousness behind the chuckle was undeniable. The fear of a new way of being, which would require a new way of living and interacting, was frightening.

"You know a new way of being requires a new way of living and interacting." I decided to interject.

She breathed in, words formed on her lips, but they went unspoken. All she could muster was an, "Umm hmm."

Then after a period of silence she said, "So, I realize working with you and writing other books that there is a common thread that weaves in and out of my stories. When I give you a story, I realize I go to a certain point and stop. Years ago, I danced. I did ballet, tap, African, I did it all. Dare I say that I was amazing. I can remember a time when my dance teacher wanted me to be on *Star Search*. Then I stopped. My success, the pinnacle of what I deem as the success mark is where I stop. I stop because that is the point where I feel I will lose all control. I do it with everything. I did it with my first house with him. I didn't want a house past the two-bedroom we bought. In my eyes it was success, or so I pretended, and I didn't want more. Having more meant I would have to be seen and being seen meant I would be like that four-year-old girl that was on full, naked display to that grown man. So, I stop even to my own detriment, even to the extent of my family.

"This is something that...that I battled my whole life. So, I'm always fighting for my fucking life. I must fight to win, to break free, so that person no longer has that control over me. It's why I get frustrated when I rely on other people and they don't work with the same sense of urgency. It's not their fault though; they don't understand the shit I walk with. This thing I battle is so much bigger than selling books. It's bigger than getting books on a table. It's bigger than a butterfly."

And just like that she was done. We reached a place where she could recognize the common threads. The control and the exposure created a life-long battle that was exasperated by her relationships and her marriage. Her need to conveniently hide behind a life she carefully crafted for her audience was becoming undone by her willingness to be exposed and no longer in control of the outcomes. It was her taking her success out of her own box so she could see just how far she could go. It was her putting on the glasses with each conversation so she could stop being afraid of the clarity, so she could live a new way of life without the blurred vision.

Patterns

"You ready?"

"Yea, I'm ready," I responded.

"So, two things. I realize that going through my bout with depression that I don't share and I'm still that little girl at times. Marcus asked why I didn't tell him how I was feeling. All I could say was, 'I'm not the one who gets depressed.' I spend my life not sharing myself. Not because I'm this massively private person but because it was ingrained. It's the four-year-old who was taught to hold her shit. Whenever anything is uncomfortable or causing me anger or angst I shut down. I'm carrying every single bag of all types of shit and I can't carry not one more freaking bag!

"I feel like my life mimicked my mom's so much. More than I care to admit. It's like I'm living her life. I married my father. My dad always had a girlfriend, my ex-husband always had a girlfriend. I think about why I married him and all I can come up with is I felt like I couldn't say no. His girlfriends were always present. I had an abortion, and he was in the car with our children talking to his girlfriend. I'm still in the hospital after having our third child and he's outside texting his girlfriend about the baby boy we just had."

At that point everything she said came out quietly between clenched teeth. I could only infer that her teeth were tightly held together so her inner rage at the events she was re-examining concerning her life didn't come out and scorch everything she had tried to build.

"I feel like I need to get this shit out so I can let this shit go. I needed a moment to say, 'No, you're not doing this shit to me again.' These are those moments. It sucks. It just sucks, but that's where I am."

"Hmmm...yea," is all I could say.

"I want to say being with him made me stronger, but I don't know if it did. I think maybe it just showed me how strong I am.

"The part of this that haunts me more than anything is that my children watched me deal with this shit. That's the part that still breaks my heart. I've talked to them about it, and I know they don't resent me. Symone says she's not angry, but you know that look in your baby's eyes when they are questioning, 'Why are you letting him talk to you like that. Why aren't you saying anything back?' I remember seeing that so many times.

"I can forgive him all these years later, but I struggle with forgiving myself for that shit. These are the points in time when I question who I was as a mother.

"That's all I got girlie."

Morning Call

The holiday season had begun. The busyness that comes with that time of year put her project on hold. The holidays have a way of doing just that, bringing everything to a screeching halt. Between school parties and concerts, family gatherings, seasonal shopping, work events, it seems that time of year has a way of bringing even the most scheduled life to a pause. So, when she called early morning during my morning commute, I shouldn't have been surprised by what she said.

As soon as I felt my phone vibrate, I answered.

"Hey, chick! What's up?"

"Chick, I am going to send you some stuff. He woke me up this morning to write. I tried to hold off on it and wait 'til we spoke, but He wasn't having it. I felt like it was bubbling inside and I had to get it out."

The *He* she was talking about was God. It's easy to understand because we share the same faith and believe that the nudge in our spirit is His way of directing us, especially when our world feels like it's moving away from our path.

I usually don't adjust to changes in the current flow of things well, but this seemed like it might be a welcomed breath of air. To not have to write every conversation just to put in story form seemed like it may be just what I needed for the mental relief as well as the emotional tug of war I felt when I heard her story and then having to place myself back there when it was time to put it to paper. I'd been in my profession for many years and had seen some horrific stories, but it never matters. Every time someone unleashes their emotional baggage you will have to be in that space with them. You must be there long enough to be present and you must be

29

skilled enough to take their weight (if they are relinquishing it) and move it away from you so there is no transference of energy. Most folk aren't skilled enough to do it which is why "few are chosen."

She continued, "Crazy thing is He is bringing stuff to the surface that I forgot about. Crazy, right?"

"I could see that." I replied.

"I didn't reread it to check for errors or flow; as it came is how I wrote it," she giggled as she spoke, underestimating her own writing ability.

"I got you. No need to worry about errors and I'll clean up any flow. This helps me, Him having you write. It should be easy enough to incorporate. We can keep your voice but change the space of how the information is being relayed. It may be a nice change for the reader."

"You sure?" She was hesitant.

"He told you to write, right?"

"Yes."

"Then we move the way He directed. You hear from Him and I'm sure of that. If He said you need to write, there is a reason. It's not up to us to question it. If He tells my spirit anything differently, I'll let you know. Until then, send me what you got."

"I'm close to the job, so I'll have to call you back."

"Cool beans, girlie. We'll talk soon."

He Woke Me Up to Write

He woke me up at 3:45 am. I say *He* because that's what *He* is to me. The *He* I am talking about is God. Nowadays you have so many terms for everything, so many politically correct ways of describing God, but to me God is just *God* and *He*. This isn't the first time He's awakened me in the wee hours of the morning, but this is the first time in a while when I couldn't just sit in that space with Him and then go back to sleep easily. I prayed. I prayed for peace in my relationships, clarity for the space I was in, and prayed for everyone I thought He woke me up for, but I still couldn't go back to sleep. I was exhausted from continually trying my hands at different things over the last few months. I had been writing and self-published a few books. I had a few speaking engagements, I was still actively being a mom, I'd begun life-coaching and the company I'd worked for during the last twenty years folded which was why I was even trying to do things I always wished I could explore. So now to be up since 3:45 am trying to figure out why God would wake me when I was trying hard to hold it together in this part of my life journey was beyond me. At some point I stopped trying to figure it out and just laid in bed staring at the ceiling waiting. As I laid there and just stared, I could feel an abundance of different emotions begin to well up inside me. It was building with intensity, touching every nerve in my body. If the emotions were water and I was the dam, then I was close to exploding at any moment. That's when I heard it in my inner-being.

"Write." One word, but crystal clear.

'*It can wait 'til I talk to Kim,*' I thought.

"No, write now," He replied.

'*It's late/early. I just want some rest...I don't want to go downstairs.*'

"Go now." The last reply felt more like a command than a request. So, I put on my robe and went downstairs to write. I wrote everything that bubbled up, every thought that came to mind. I didn't worry about whether it made sense, if it was in order, if it was spelled correctly, I just wrote it all down until I felt empty. I wrote until all those emotions left and when relief washed over me, I knew I was done. Then at that moment I felt exhausted, like I could lay on my floor and sleep. So, I shut my laptop and turned off the light. I walked up each step slowly and climbed in bed next to my husband and slept like a baby.

The Four-Year-Old Me Became Six...and Then Eight

She sent over the first entry that she wrote. She's not a seasoned writer so I wasn't sure what she would send. I wasn't sure if it would be enough. Yet I knew He told her to write, and who was I to question what she was sure of. Would she repeat anything she already told me? Would she give a different account, a different spin? Molestation and abuse, both physical and emotional, are heavy topics, so I opened the email and began to read.

"Most of my life was lived in fear. Fear of who was going to attack me next. I can remember snippets of the first time. I told her about it already, but only in pieces. There's a part of my brain that won't allow me to recall everything and it's probably best. To be honest I am ok with not remembering all of it, but I remember being four. I remember the house of my babysitter and the layout. There was an upstairs and downstairs. It was well-kept and medium in size, at least that's how I saw it from my four-year-old eyes. I remember the first time we went to her house. I was in my dad's car. His car was brown with big leather back seats. I was in the backseat that day listening to 'For the Love of Money,' by the O'Jays as I looked out the window without a care in the world. I can remember both my parents being in the front seat while we drove to this lady's house. The lady who would be my sitter until school started. They told me she had two sons and one was around my age, which was good because it meant I had someone to play with. I don't recall how long it took for her oldest son to notice me, but I don't think it was long. I can remember being in the bathtub and whenever he came into the bathroom I would instinctively stand up and right when he would begin to...

At this point my mind goes blank, I don't want to remember all that happened, so I let it go dark. I can feel the tears fall at the memory of standing in that bathtub, naked and afraid. I see the teardrops hit the keyboard as I typed. I can still see that 4-year-old with her slightly pot belly, flat chest, knobby knees, standing in that bathtub alone. Never knowing what to say, just knowing I was afraid. I feel that fear with each memory.

"I can remember the bedroom where *it* would happen. It's always interesting to me what you remember when shit happens to you.

"The room wasn't that big. When you walked in, the bed was to the left of the door against a dingy wall. I know it was dingy because it's grayish and not the gray everyone is painting their walls now. The bed was a twin and made up in a haphazard type of way. There were always toys in the room, probably to keep his little brother 'entertained' while he did what he wanted to me. The carpet on the floor was a deep burgundy and dirty. I remember this because I would look at that floor every time he told me to step out of my overalls and hope it would swallow me up. He always told me how nice I looked and how much he liked me. I remember being reminded by him and every other adult that I was a kid and should be obedient and listen to my elders. Looking back, I realize he was nowhere near the elders I was taught to listen to, but when you're four, eighteen looks like a person I am supposed to listen to. I can remember him always placing my panties under the pillow. I remember the first time he came in my hand. I had no idea what it was, but I kept thinking about how gross it was and wondering why he had to do it all over my hand. I often think about how I went from a talkative kid to barely saying a word. It's crazy because when you have parents that are just trying to make ends meet, having a 'quiet, well-behaved' child was their blessing. Not once did they notice the shift in my personality or my movements. That thing with him went on the entire summer and I never told. I was the obedient child they said I should be and because they never countered that rule with 'if someone touches you inappropriately, make sure you tell,' I never told. I kept it a secret and that secret would shape, alter, and dictate most of my entire life.

"He wasn't the last. From ages 4 to 8, people chose me, directed me, instructed me, positioned me, and decided for me. I remember spending the night at the home of a family friend. I was told they were my cousins, but they were just extended family and not blood related at all. The kids were twin girls and they had bunk beds which I had never seen so imagine my excitement at sleeping on the top bunk. The first night the twins slept on the bottom while I slept on the top. It took a while, but once the excitement of being at my first sleepover began to wear off, I fell asleep. When I woke up one of the twins was lying next to me. I kept my eyes closed in the hope that what she was doing would stop. It didn't and instead her sister came up and got in bed as well. I opened my eyes and never said a word. I was gripped with a fear I still have no words for to this day. I did as they said. 'Touch me here.' 'Kiss me back.' When they finally returned to their bunk, I just laid there not moving, not making a sound. The next morning my 'aunt' came to tell us she had errands to run and we would stay at the house. She left them in charge. Once she left, they told me to follow them. I thought maybe they would tell me not to tell anyone about what they did. I thought they would say something like what he said, when I was four. Little did I know...

"I followed them through the kitchen into the backyard. We all still had on our nightgowns. It was cool out. The grass was still damp from dew, so it sank ever so slightly with each step. My knobby knees hit each other as I walked, partly because I was afraid. I knew they had a dog, but I didn't see it. We walked towards a wooden pole, probably the size of a 2x4, in the middle of the yard. One of the girls grabbed me by my shoulders and shoved me against the pole. She then took out a rope and began to tie me to the pole. As the tears began to form, I noticed the other girl coming out the broken-down garage with the dog. The dog was mean. He only seemed to like them, and I was afraid, deathly afraid. That's when she said, 'You better not tell anyone what we did or we gon' let this dog go! Ya hear?!'

"I was six years old. All I could do was nod my head and cry. To this day I hate grass and I avoid it whenever I can. Interestingly enough, it is at this very moment that I just realized that's the reason I hate grass.

"By the time I was eight, I was touched for the last time. I went to my mother and simply said, 'The janitor kissed me today and I didn't like it.' It never dawned on me that being touched in this way was a bad thing. I only mentioned it to my mom because his mouth covered mine and it felt yucky. Him pulling me from the hallway and into the stairwell annoyed me because he pulled me away from my friends. But I wondered if I did like it, would I have told? How does an 8-year-old know what they like and what they don't when their hormones haven't even changed over? I don't know, and never will at this point, but this shit is crazy because no child should ever get used to this being their norm. No childhood should ever end at four."

Why Didn't He Love Me

Another one came through the very next day. I opened the email and began to skim. I was looking for parts I would need clarification on and parts I would need to clean up for the final draft. In my skimming, I came across the line, "Fear of never seeing my father and him never really loving me."

It made me pause. Although I wasn't what you call the quintessential "daddy's girl," I grew up with my dad and I knew with all his faults he loved me with every fiber in his being. So, I stopped skimming for the things I may need to clean up and just read. As I did, I could hear her voice in every line.

"There were so many days I spent sitting by the window with my coat on, sweat running down my face, while I waited for him to come, but he never did. Day after day, month after month, year after year, I sat by that window in our walk-up apartment in the city and waited. I waited for my knight in shining armor. I waited for that man that would kiss every tear and tell me how much he loved me. I waited for a girl's first love. I waited for my dad. After a while, my mom stopped telling me to take off my coat and she never dared say he wasn't coming. She knew one day I'd stop waiting; I didn't know when I'd stop waiting. I think I stopped when I no longer wore my coat while I waited. I had decided I would wait until he got there to put my coat on. I figured I could still wait for him; I just wouldn't sweat while I waited. I don't remember when I stopped waiting at that window, but eventually I did. I stopped believing and slowly, I came to the realization that he was never coming. Then with a completely broken heart and defeated spirit, I stopped asking about him altogether.

"One day, years later, he called out of the blue. I don't remember what I was doing when the phone rang but I remember answering it. Back then everyone didn't have phones so if you had a house phone and it rang, it was because someone you knew was calling for a reason. That day it was my father. My heart skipped at the sound of his voice. I smiled ear to ear because he called. Finally!

'Hey Dad!'

"I couldn't contain the excitement I felt. You could hear it in my voice. It's the excitement you hear when a 5-year-old sees all the gifts she's wanted all year under the Christmas tree.

"Anyone on the outside never would have guessed that we didn't speak. They never would have guessed how long I waited for him to call if they heard us on the phone. It was like he never missed coming to get me. Like I never waited. It was a dream come true moment only I knew instinctively that it was just a moment. At that moment, I wanted so badly to have a relationship with him. I wanted that relationship where teenage girls call their dads and ask advice. I wanted to be his baby girl. I wanted that call where he would say, 'I'm on my way,' and then he would show up. So, I sat on the phone and waited in expectancy to see if that was that day.

"'Shanice,' he said in a tone that let me know he was upset. I look back at that moment and realize that you can go years without speaking to someone, but if they're angry, it is unmistakable. You hear it in their voice, in their tone. Then he asked the unthinkable.

'Shanice...why am I paying child support?'

"I was stunned by the question. I could say I was confused but it was more than that. It was a hurt that cut so deeply that it hit the bone marrow. It's the kind of hurt your soul never forgets. He then hit me with a barrage of questions laced with anger that I could not wrap my head around. I felt my skin grow hot and the tears began to fall. I had no answers for his questions and all I could do was stumble over each one. *'I'm your daughter!'* I thought. *'I don't even know about any child support, what is he talking about?'* I couldn't process the things he was saying because it was so far from what I'd hoped he'd say.

"My mom saw my tears and the look on my face, and she snatched the phone from me.

'Hello!' she said in that stern, yet protective, mommy way. It was clear that Mommy was going to shred whoever was making her baby girl cry.

'Who is this?!' she shouted. And then she heard him and stopped. He didn't realize she'd taken the phone, but she got the gist of what he'd said to me and she lost it! Every bit of her Caribbean accent came out through clenched teeth.

'Gavin, you calling this child to yell at her about child support?! Wha de ass is wrong wit you?? You have to pay child support for this chile! You don't call my fucking house and question her about what I do! Do you even love Shanice?!'

"At the sound of that question, I whipped my head around and looked at her. She asked the question I'd been asking myself all these years. She was getting the answer I'd been waiting to hear. Only it wasn't the answer I wanted. I saw it on her face. The hurt on her face matched the feeling in my heart. The feeling I'd been carrying since I was little. The one man that was supposed to love me unconditionally didn't. He was supposed to love me with no strings attached because I was a part of him. I was devastated. It was one of the biggest *fuck yous* I'd ever felt without the person actually saying it. It was as if the creation of me was just something to do because he planted his seed, stayed around for my first five years, and bounced, never looking back. At that moment, I changed forever. I guess anyone would. It was that moment of realizing that the fear of never seeing my father and the bigger issue of him never really loving me came to fruition. How do you go back after that? How could we still build a relationship when it wasn't based on any kind of mutual feelings? Our feelings were so opposite.

"So, I walked away that day. My heart walked away from that feeling, that pain. It never left me really. It always sits in the shadows of my life hoping I'll acknowledge it, but I can't. I won't. If I did, I'd be that 7-year-old girl with a coat on, sweating by the window waiting for my first love to show up. So, I walked away from the window never to return to that spot again."

Lisa V. Taitt-Stevenson

Images

The next entry came. It was longer than any of the previous ones. At first glance, I could see and feel the pain coming at me with each sentence. One word that hit my soul and stayed with me all day was *images.* It made me think about the images people portray. The image they often put out to the world about themselves, their families, their careers, etc. The image is never really the truth of their life. It's often what's behind the image that shows the truth. The truth about what's going on in their life, in their soul. So, I read, looking to see her truth, her soul. What I saw made me remember my own image and the truths that were behind them.

"He loved the image of his family and how it made him look. He didn't love me though. Hell, he didn't even like me. Even now it breaks my heart to think about it. Each night I laid down with a man who talked to me like I was just some random he met on the corner, like a trick on the street. I love my kids dearly, but I often wonder how I had kids with the same man who would see me sick in bed and ask, 'Is this what you did all day? Stay in the bed?' He showed no sympathy, no empathy, no compassion, no kindness. Each time I nursed myself back to health and went through the motions. I almost chuckle at the thought of 'nursing myself back to health' because in reality how healthy can you be when you're in a toxic relationship. I ate the foods *he thought* I should eat. I wore the clothes *he thought* looked best on me, which fed into the image he wanted seen. I wore hairstyles *he approved* of. I kept my weight down and stayed fit just the way *he wanted.* My life was his. This is probably why the thought of all I left behind still brings tears to my eyes. There were so many years of hurt. Years where I just wanted to be held, to be kissed, to be loved...hell to just be liked. I can only shake my head when I think of my ex-husband. In public, in front of others he did all those things, but behind closed doors I got the real him. The one that didn't give two shits about me. See outside, we appeared to be *that couple*. The one our friends envied; the couple our friends strived to be. When we went out, he smiled, I smiled, and we played our respective parts, but when we got home, we went our separate ways. I can remember getting headaches whenever we were on our way home. The headaches came from the tension between us, the anticipation of the loneliness and isolation that was sure to come as soon as we stepped through the door.

I knew he scrutinized everything I did. *'Why are you cooking it like that?'* *'Do that this way.'* *'Why are you moving left? Move right.'* It didn't matter what I did or how I did it because he always had a better way. This way of living left me feeling smaller and smaller each day."

I imagined she paused here. She paused to collect her thoughts. Maybe even wipe her tears. She paused to remember the pain so she could write it from that space. That moment where she could feel every feeling like she was in it all over again.

"I look back on the photos from then and see how tiny I was. I was so thin. Petite. My weight was the envy of everyone I knew, but little did they know. I can see how sad my eyes looked in the pictures. I was smiling in many of them, but I knew then like I know now what I was hiding. When I think about it, I'm surprised I didn't have a nervous breakdown. I spent so many nights crying out to God. Each time I cried and screamed in my pillow so my kids couldn't hear me. He wasn't home so it didn't matter. Interestingly enough, years later my oldest child shared with me that she heard my cries.

"I remember one evening I went outside to his truck to look for something. I don't remember what I was looking for, but I do remember finding condoms in the console. I threw them away. Now that I think about it, that shit was funny. I figured since he was getting sloppy about his cheating, I would eventually figure out who *she* was. That same night I put the kids down for bed and decided to turn in early. I laugh now as I remember him saying he had 'plans with the boys that night,' only to be awakened by the sound of him frantically going through my drawers at two o'clock in the morning. I immediately knew what he was doing.

I smiled and stifled a laugh as I asked him, 'What are you looking for?' He didn't tell me; I didn't expect him to. I felt so victorious in that moment. I wanted to shout, 'You dumb ass, why would you leave a box of condoms in your car?! Hey stupid, I know what you are looking for and guess what? I threw them shits away!' But I kept those thoughts to myself. Instead, he said, 'I'm just looking for something.' I mustered up a response with as much fake ass concern as I could and said, 'Well maybe if you tell me what it is, I can help you find it.' He said, 'Never mind,' and a few minutes later gave up his frantic search. I simply said, 'Okay' and rolled back over to go back to sleep. I tried hard to contain my laughter at that fool looking for those damn condoms like a crackhead searching for something to sell. Shit was hilarious. I couldn't even get mad anymore because that was our norm.

"My grandma used to always say, 'Don't take a torchlight to look for something in the dark that you can see in the light.' Low and behold, the riddle was solved the next day. The same console I found the condoms in the night before had a receipt from a hotel for the previous night. Looking at the receipt my heart fell. I was used to his cheating. I expected him to, but this was a friend. A close friend. You see the receipt had her name on it because the room was booked in her name and he paid the bill which is why he had it. At that moment I felt so many emotions that I probably needed to work through with betrayal being the strongest. She was my friend and her blatant disregard caught me by surprise. I felt a rage I had never known burn deep. That rage was all consuming and engulfed me quickly. So, I called her. She didn't answer so I did what anyone else would. *67 to the rescue. She may not answer my number, but she will answer a blocked call. And answer she did.

"'Hello Deena,' I said in the calmest voice I could muster. I was numb to all the shenanigans and the shit was comical, but now my battle wasn't just him and a bunch of randoms. She was a friend or at least someone I believed was a friend.

"She sighed and said, 'Hello.' I asked how she was, and she reluctantly said she was okay. I knew she was bracing herself for the question that was coming so instead I said, 'I've been calling you, Why didn't you answer?'

'He told me not to.' That was her reply. I had to laugh out loud at that one.

'He told you not to answer my calls? Are you fucking kidding me?' I wasn't really asking her, but more so repeating out loud what she'd just said.

Clearly oblivious to my rhetorical question, she confirmed with a yes. So, I went in at that point.

'You know why I'm calling you, right?' That was the question, I wanted her to answer. I knew the answer but if she was doing it, she should be bold enough to admit it.

'Yes,' she said.

'Great, so you sleeping with my husband now?' I didn't wait for her to answer; I just went right in.

'I've had you in my home, around my kids, and you do this?! Why?! You didn't think I would find out?! Let me make this clear. I find out about all the women he sleeps with.'

Up until that point she was silent, ready for what I would say. Maybe she knew she deserved it, maybe she didn't care, but once she heard me say *all the women*, her interest was piqued.

'Wait there were others?' she asked. I could hear the hurt behind her question.

'Are you flipping kidding me right now?! You catching feelings? You mad he has others? You are just a piece of ass to him. You think he wants to be with you beyond that hotel room? He didn't want us talking because he didn't want you to know what he was doing. It has nothing to do with me finding out. You aren't the first and won't be the last. Welcome to my world.' I chuckled out loud at her stupidity, yet at the same time I felt sorry for her because of her naivety.

I asked her, 'How long has this been going on?'

'Just a few months.'

'You plan on continuing with him?'

'Well...'

I slapped myself on the forehead. I was clearly in the twilight zone and we all looked crazy. *This trick just said she wants to continue, she's in love or at least she thinks she is.* I'm done so I moved on.

'Goodbye Deena.' I hung up. No tears, no heartache, just another nail in an impending coffin that is going to house and bury this sham of a marriage."

She was done with this one. I could tell the way it ended. There was nothing else on the entry and nothing in the next one that referenced this one. She said no heartache but it's more of a heart that has been calloused from hurt. That situation created another layer of skin to cover an organ that is supposed to feel and love. As the old timers say, "No one can touch the pain of a heart that's been broken." And in Shanice's case, it was beyond repair, so I moved on to the next.

The Day I Faced My Own Destruction

It had been a week since I received an entry from her. I could only assume it was taking some time because they were so personal, diary-like. Whenever someone is revealing parts of themselves that are so intimate, it takes time. She needed to take her time with each piece. She had to sit in that space, the one that would allow her to peel all the layers back as she wrote. I figured that was why it took so long to receive this entry.

It arrived in my inbox late at night, but I didn't see it until the early morning hours. The first thing I noticed was the title: "The Day I Faced My Own Destruction." The title implied that something was destroyed. It could be anything, an object, a person...but knowing her the way I did, I assumed a piece of her soul was destroyed. A piece that would be difficult to heal. I took a deep breath and opened the attachment. What was written was something that seemed unreal but I knew it was her raw truth.

"I'm not sure why I kept asking him about things I'd find, but I did. I always hoped he would answer truthfully even though he didn't. I often wondered if he could be truthful. He lied so much I don't think he knew the difference.

'Whose such and such?' I would ask. His response would never be the truth. He would always give a different version of a previous lie. Usually his responses went something like, 'I don't know what you are talking about.' 'Oh, she's just someone that wants to rent out an apartment' 'Oh, my boy is talking to her.' It was always some bullshit that although I couldn't prove at that moment, I knew it wasn't the truth. I knew even if he was honest it wouldn't change anything. I would eventually need to leave, but I still hoped. I hoped for honesty, for change, for something better.

One day I was in the basement going through a basket of fresh laundry looking for some items to wear to work. It was a Monday. He came downstairs and at that moment, I decided to ask him about Deena. I'm not sure why I asked. I hadn't mentioned it to him previously even though I was sure he already knew we had spoken. Maybe I was hoping for honesty. Maybe understanding. Possibly both. I don't know but I asked anyway.

'Did you sleep with Deena?'

He stopped looking for whatever he came down there to find. I could see his body grow stiff with anger. I took a step back because it looked like something in him cracked wide open. He balled up his fist, reached back and punched a hole in the wall. I couldn't move. With everything we'd been through this seemed to be the angriest I'd ever seen him. I stayed in that spot. Part of me was shocked, the other part of me was making decisions. Decisions I'd been pondering for a long time but wasn't gutsy enough to take. Decisions I always second guessed in the face of hope. That day was different though. That day I said out loud what was running through my mind. I didn't say it with a raised voice though. It was more to myself and wasn't above a whisper, so I didn't think he heard it. I was wrong.

'I have to go. I have to leave him.'

Those two short sentences, that were barely even a whisper, were changing all the pieces in and around me. He looked at me with an expression that seemed shocked. At that moment I knew he heard me. I wasn't sure what he was going to say or do for that matter, so I stood there.

'Shanice, why are you doing this? Why do you keep looking through my phone? Why are you always accusing me?' His voice grew louder and angrier with each question.

'Shanice, do you want to see what destruction looks like?! I'm going to show you destruction! Symone, Isaiah, get down here!" He was calling our children downstairs. Our children came downstairs with mixed expressions on their faces. I couldn't tell if it was fear or confusion.

"Yes daddy?" they replied.

At that moment he looked at me with hate and stated, "Mommy wants to divorce Daddy because Mommy thinks Daddy loves other women."

He hit me in a place that went down deep because he brought them into it. He told them what I was thinking and knew they wouldn't understand. I saw my babies' expressions move from bewildered to pain and then they cried. Their cries came from the deepest part of them. A place that can only be described as a broken heart. In that moment, their world was completely shattered, and Daddy told them it was Mommy's fault because I wanted to leave. I was destroyed. He put his hand on each of their little shoulders, looked me in my eyes and said, 'Now tell them that we are going to work it out. Tell them that you won't divorce me and that we are going to work it out.'

Checkmate.

I stood there seeing both their faces clearly. He looked victorious and they looked hopeful as they waited for my answer. I looked at my babies tear-streaked faces and heard them hold their breath as they waited for my next words.

'Yes my loves, Daddy and I are going to work it out.'

As I said those words and saw relief wash over their faces, I knew it was not over. It was checkmate at the moment, but it wouldn't stay that way. I no longer needed the truth; I needed a plan because we were all roped in. If I stayed, destruction would surely come so I started looking for a way out.

$\mathcal{S}$*takeout*

"Hey, chick."

I called her to discuss the direction I thought she should take with the next entry. I wasn't sure how she would feel about what I wanted her to write about so I needed to be cautious in my request. Although it was a story we both shared a laugh or two about, it was still a painful part of her past. It was only funny at this point because she had moved on with her life and whenever she retold the story it played out like a Lifetime movie in real time. Yet, no matter how many times we may chuckle at it now, it was not funny when it was happening to her.

"I think there is one more story you should share before we end the time spent on your ex-husband. I know it's sensitive in nature and you are extremely private but it's one of those stories that shows the depth of what it means to be trapped in a sham of a marriage. So I'd like you to share the story about the stakeout. Just the fact that we've both laughed over the replay shows people that bad things can happen, but everyone has the ability to move past those incidents and eventually find happiness if they choose. Just think about it."

We hung up and I gave her space to think about it. Two days later she sent an entry entitled "Stakeout." I opened the document and chuckled. She began her entry almost where we left off in our phone conversation.

******

She asked me to write this. I wasn't sure if I wanted to share it, but as a good example of what we do as sister-friends, I felt like I had to share this one. You see for every story on sisterhood that's about one sister looking out for another there is always that one story everyone can relate to but won't necessarily share with others, except a chosen few. Well, I have one such story, and I remember it like it was yesterday. It makes me laugh now but at the time when it was going down, it was some real shit.

Eric and I were struggling in our marriage. He was cheating and instead of owning his indiscretions he tried to make me believe I was crazy for "accusing" him. This had been going on for years, to the point where it wasn't even off and on, rather it was just always on. I shed many tears, prayed many prayers, argued many times, and got to the point where, dare I say, tried to accept it as just a part of him. That didn't work, and it took me to my breaking point. I was ready to end the marriage. I was tired, beat down and surprised I was standing at that point. Since he always said, "You've haven't caught me; you have no proof," my prayer changed from, *'God, fix this'* to *'God, give me proof so I can be done. Let me catch him so this farce of a marriage can be over.'* Now, I won't say it was God who gave me this. Perhaps it was the devil, but that day would eventually come.

One day I got home early from work and was in my kitchen when I heard the phone buzz alerting me of a text message. I looked at the phone and a message from a number I didn't recognize popped up.

Tomorrow at 3 is fine.

I stood there confused at first. *Three...what the heck did I schedule?* Then I realized that I wasn't looking at my phone but his. We had the same phone and the same case. He wasn't home so he must've accidentally left it. I immediately had a thought. It was my opportunity. I didn't mention it to him when he got home and moved around the house the way I usually do. When he had a chance to look at his phone he asked, "Are the kids home tomorrow?" I very innocently, almost playfully, asked him why. He stated that he was just wondering.

Yea, ok. I just looked at him. I immediately started putting my plan in motion.

"Yeah, the kids have school and by the way, you won't be able to contact me at all tomorrow as we have an audit going on at work. I'll also need to leave the house earlier than usual to get there on time."

He bought it with no questions asked. Fortunately for me that type of thing wasn't out of the norm. It just didn't happen at that time of the year, but he never paid attention to my work schedule. I moved quickly because the opportunity may never happen again if he caught on. I ran upstairs and called my girl. When she answered I said, "Listen, I need you to meet me where I park my car and then bring me back home."

She didn't ask why, she just said, "Ok, what time do you need me there?" *Damn, I love her!* She was *that* girl, and I knew that from day one when we met.

The next morning couldn't come fast enough. I woke, showered, dressed, and hightailed it out of the house ready to get on with my mission. I parked my car at the spot and there was my girl waiting for me. As we rode back to my house, I explained everything that was going on. As she drove, I put the seat all the way back so if we passed him on the road he couldn't see me. Low and behold, he passed us as he was taking the kids to school. I promised her I would keep in contact by texts as much as I could. I couldn't believe I was sneaking back in my house to hide. As ready as I was though, I was nervous and a part of me hoped I was wrong about what I thought was going to happen.

After an hour he came home...alone! *Wait he's alone...dammit! I took the day off work to do this and it's not going down?! But the text did say 3, so maybe she's coming later.* So, I waited. I really didn't have a choice at that point. I had snacks with me in my hideout, so I was good!

Tick-tock. Tick-tock. Time moved at a snail's pace, but then I heard the shower and talking. *Did she come in and I missed it?* I heard his voice, but I didn't hear hers, so I tiptoed down the stairs and listened hard! Thank God for carpeting! What I heard was just as nutty as the whole stakeout; he was having an entire conversation about me with himself.

"Oh, this bitch thinks I'm cheating, huh? Oh, she not gon' give me none. Yeah, ok."

I turned around at that point to head back to the hideout. I was waiting for the action. When I heard the water stop, I ran upstairs to my spot. He got dressed and left the house again. This time I was sure he'd be back with her.

Tick-tock. Tick-tock... The waiting was driving me crazy. Finally, I looked out the window and I saw him. *Wait—what the hell is he doing with my car?! Oh shit! He's not alone!* He went to my parking spot and got my car. *What the hell is that about! I'll have to figure that shit out another time.* I had to focus on what was happening in real time. I watched him walk in the house with her. And just as I thought, she had on a hood so no one could see her face. When they walked in, they headed straight for the basement.

Now I had two options. Go down right away and yell, "Aha! I got you muthafucka!" Or I could wait 'til they really got into it because the first option would leave him an opportunity to talk his way out of it. So, I waited again. I waited long enough for them to get started. I started to slowly make my way downstairs until I got to the basement. And just like I thought they were getting it in. I laugh now thinking about the lengths we will go to catch our significant other out there.

He was kneeling in front of her, kissing her passionately. Her legs were wrapped around his waist and he was palming her ass and slamming into her. They didn't see or hear me sitting across from them in his recliner. I sat there while they went at it until they noticed me.

Mid-stroke, she opened her eyes and saw me. The look on her face was one of shock, confusion, and mortification all in one. I was laughing on the inside. *Un-freaking-believable*! She put her hand on his chest to stop him.

"What?" He was confused by her sudden motion to stop.

"It's your wife."

That's where I lost it. I lost it because she said, "It's your wife." I lost it because she didn't think I was a stranger. She knew exactly who I was even though I didn't know her. She knew he had a flipping wife!

I stood up and said, "Yes, bitch. It's his wife." At the same time the voice in my head said, *'This is what you wanted, remember?'* So, I stepped behind the recliner because I had 3 children to consider and to lose my shit completely meant I may lose them too. The voice was right though, this was exactly what I wanted. I stayed behind the recliner and let the feeling of relief wash over me. Relief because I was finally validated. I no longer had to hear him say I was the crazy one because his ass was caught in the act. And with that, I could be out!

The girl got up and got dressed. She nervously shook the entire time. He, being the piece of work he was, looked at me like, *'How dare you interrupt my fuck session and cut it short.'* He apologized to *her* and drove *her* home in *my* car. I told you he was a piece of shit!

When they left I exhaled. I exhaled because I was free from the speculation space he created with the constant denials. I was free from the, "it wasn't me" bullshit. I was free to move with no regret.

So, when you ask why I can laugh at all of this, let me explain. I bet she gets flashbacks every time she thinks about that basement or any basement for that matter. And with all his bravado that day, that muthafucka damn near had a heart attack when he came back home, and I said my ass was out. I mean, why get mad? You and your shit lasted longer than most sitcoms. *Time to drop the mic. Deuces my dude. I'm out!*

A New Day For All

I left weeks before my 40th birthday. I left wondering if I could do it. Could I make it on my own? I was afraid and excited at that same time. I told him we that needed some space. I think I may have phrased it as some time apart so we could be on the same page and move forward as a family unit. I told him it was temporary and that the kids needed to be in a better school system. I told him after we sold the house, he would move with us and we would all be together again under one roof. I told him it was the way to keep our family together so we could move forward with our dream. I told him all of the things I knew his ego and image needed. I told him whatever I thought he wanted to hear so I could leave. I told everyone we knew that we were separating only physically so he could pursue some things to help our family, and I was moving with the kids to a better school district to set up our new life so when we all came back together under one roof the transition would be easy. I made our future life look perfect. We were still the envy of our circle. People are gullible when they think you've got something they want. They refuse to see that not only is the grass not greener, but there ain't no damn grass! I probably should have gone into acting with that performance. He believed me because he was the liar in the family, and I was the always honest yet weak, obedient wife. Our friends believed it because why wouldn't they? We were the "perfect" family and Shanice always told the truth and always had the right answer to every situation.

The day I left, I hugged him goodbye and whispered, "We just need some space." I played my part all the way through to the end. I may have even let him see a glimmer of tears forming just for fucks sake. Once I got in my car though, I knew I wasn't going back, not if my life depended on it...and it did. The moving truck even had a hard time following me once we were out of his visual. I couldn't get to my new apartment fast enough. I drove with urgency, with purpose. I smiled at myself and moved with a new determination. I had never experienced this feeling. I moved like a woman, not a child. I moved with certainty, and I moved on my own terms, something I hadn't done in over 15 years. I didn't take much with me. Just the clothes, my children's furniture and one of the couches. I really didn't care about where I slept; all that mattered was that it was under my own roof.

Turning Forty

In my newfound freedom, my new chapter, I had some time to reflect about where I'd been and where I was headed. I sat in my apartment and remembered there was a time in my life I think I spent more time on my knees praying than anything else. I cried out to God every day. At home, at work, in the car, no place was off limits. Oftentimes at night, I would fall asleep mid-cry, only to wake up in the same spot I laid in to cry out again. I'm surprised I didn't have permanent tear stains on my face. I would ask God, *"What happened to joy coming in the morning?"* I'd heard all the scriptures, songs, and sermons about joy coming in the morning, but it seemed like mine never did. I started to wonder if God even heard me. Was I too damaged to be listened to? Did He bypass my prayers because I was so tainted? I cried, I screamed, and I wailed, *"God please help me,"* because I couldn't understand the suffering. I knew that God provided miracles but for some reason the one I was looking for never came. He never fixed him. I never could admit this to anyone before but I knew that I was not supposed to marry him. I knew it when I walked down that aisle. He told me to turn around and I didn't. Instead, I said, *"God I got this,"* and got it I did...more than I imagined.

Several weeks after I'd left and was still adjusting to being on my own, I celebrated my birthday. It was my 40th, the year of change. I had just moved, and it was the beginning of the year, quite literally. Turning 40 was when everything changed for me. I already told you I was starting anew. I had some weeks of reflection that made me realize that maybe my prayers were being answered differently. I remember a certain clarity coming to my thoughts and movements. It was as if I went to bed with a light off and woke up with it on. I was beginning to shine.

I remember one day walking past my full-length mirror after getting out of the shower and pausing. I hadn't done that in so long that it seemed weird to now look at myself almost naked. I didn't want to look at myself and see the scars that were hidden from the world but very visible to me. I mean it didn't even feel like my body because for so long I had no say or control over it. I forced myself to look harder until I saw me. I saw the way my shoulders curved downward from all the years of trying to shrink myself. I saw the sadness behind my eyes and the smile lines that seemed permanently etched around my mouth from years of faking the smile just a little too hard so no one would know my truth.

I dropped my towel and I saw through my skin at the scars from emotional and verbal abuse. I saw how thin I was and what it all meant to my stature. I saw the stretch marks on my belly and the side of my breasts from each pregnancy. I saw moles and the faint markings of bruises that healed over time. As I kept looking, I noticed that I was still standing, not as tall as I would have liked but still standing, nonetheless. I noticed the rise and fall of my breasts with each breath. Those breaths revealed more life within me that I didn't know I still had. I saw the arch in my back, where my backbone and strength lived. They didn't break me. All those people didn't win. He didn't break me, even though he tried. I didn't fully know the woman who was looking back at me, but I knew she fought to be there. It was there in front of that mirror where I saw someone worth getting to know, someone worth acknowledging. It was that moment that I knew I was worth celebrating. For the first time, I saw all of me and all I wanted to do was take the time to get to know the woman who was here all along.

Freedom

The day I left my ex-husband, the day I whispered, "I'll be back" in his ear was the moment I tasted Freedom. It was like the difference between living a life in black and white and then everything moving to color. It was like seeing pasta on an all-white dinner plate to seeing it on a cobalt blue plate with a rich red sauce on top with the prettiest long stem wine glass full of what you know will be a great tasting drink indeed. Freedom offered me peace, choices, and the ability to get to know the parts of me I didn't know existed. Freedom and I became friends that day and I would hold onto her like a child holds a security blanket. Before then, I walked this life at a pace that I never really felt was my own, but with Freedom I could feel my walk turn into a jog and then a full-on sprint.

Freedom reminded me that I could finally have bacon! I remember so vividly the first time I went grocery shopping for my new apartment with Freedom walking beside me, as well as my children. It was a frigid, January morning shortly after I moved out. Usually having to go to the supermarket in cold weather felt like an annoyance, but with Freedom it was an experience I embraced to the fullest. I grabbed my cart and headed into ShopRite, kids in tow. I had to be mindful of how much I spent since I was footing the bill solo, but I was grateful to walk each aisle at my leisure and check out new items I'd never noticed before. I'm a bit of a foodie so for me the experience was like walking in a candy store for the very first time and realizing you could get whatever you want. I walked each aisle checking out so many things thinking, '*Oooh, that looks good*' and '*I must get that next time I come*', and '*I've never seen that before.*'

I had been exploring the store for almost an hour and was almost out of aisles to peruse when I saw it. Maybe it was because my ex-husband never allowed me to buy it, or maybe it was because I missed the way it smelled if Mommy cooked it on an early Saturday morning. Whatever it was, you would have thought the bacon looked like bars of chocolate wrapped in gold foil. I remember thinking, 'Wow, look at that! I remember when I could eat that,' and then I shrugged and walked past the section. I probably only got a few more feet when Freedom jumped in front of me, bringing me to a screeching halt. She quickly reminded me that I was free! It was almost as if Freedom shouted, "You are a grown ass woman, who now lives with just her children. Hell yea, you can have some damn bacon!" I hurried back to that section and grabbed three packs and then I practically ran to the checkout lane.

"I am going home and cooking some BACON!"

My shopping trip was complete and now the mission shifted to getting back home as soon as I could so I could have something my soul craved. I had bacon all week that week. I kissed it, I sang to it, I danced while eating it. See it wasn't so much the bacon as it was the Freedom to have what the fuck I wanted and how I wanted it. It was the realization that Freedom wanted me to grow, to soar, and I was ready. I was ready to take each step whether I fell or not because having the opportunity to choose for one's self is truly priceless.

Keep Writing

Shanice sent another set of writings a few weeks later. Just like the first, they were reminiscent of diary entries. The type of writings that contain your innermost thoughts, feelings, and secrets. Like the first set, they were preceded by an entry about how He woke her up in the early morning hours to get it all out. I read each entry slowly, looking for changes that would need to be made to grammar and flow. But there wasn't much there as far as errors, so I found myself drawn in, captivated by a story I thought knew only to realize that the complicated layers were full of pain I'd never experienced. As her words jumped out from each page, I knew that this project was unlike any I'd ever done or would do. She wrote this entry to me, so I would understand just where she was on each page.

"The second time He woke me up, it was 6 am and I was ready. I knew it was Him by the gentle nudge in my soul. Like the first time I prayed, but it was different. This time I listened for Him. I listened for direction with my heart. I didn't think about the why. Instead, I quieted my thoughts and sat in a space clear of clutter. Eventually the emotions and memories that would grace the next set of pieces I would send you began to bubble up in my spirit, so I went downstairs and opened my laptop. As I stared at the blue screen, it began to blur; I was crying. I could feel old wounds surface, and new realizations emerge simultaneously. I realized all these feelings had a purpose. I also realized that I wasn't alone. God was right there guiding each word, each keystroke, and carrying each tear. As I typed what I knew was my truth, I felt relief in each line. I didn't have to hide or be politically correct. I felt no shame. I sat there and watched the sun rise as

I wrote. I felt the warmth of the sun through the window on my skin. I heard my family wake up one by one. Soon after, the tears stopped falling, my fingers slowed down, and I knew I was finished. That time I didn't go back to bed; I smiled at the energy I felt moving through me. I felt lighter, like I could step on the scale and it would reflect that the weight had been removed. That was the space where I could take flight. I knew Freedom and I knew Love, but I was ready to fly to the places I hadn't already been. So, I took a breath and hit send.

The Apology

Whenever I received a call from him it always brought on a feeling of anxiety. I would be gripped with fear. I wasn't afraid for my life; I was afraid of the confrontation I knew was bound to come. So, when I saw his name pop up on my phone, I answered reluctantly. As I hit answer, my mind raced through a gamut of questions. *Did I forget something? Did I do something wrong that warranted a call?* The kids were with me, so I knew that it wasn't something that had to do with them. I took a deep breath.

"Hello."

What I heard on the other end caught me completely by surprise. He didn't sound like himself as the harshness that normally laced his tone wasn't there. The condescending way he usually said my name wasn't there. Instead, what I heard was a vulnerability and genuineness I had never experienced with him. He immediately started speaking and what he was saying was something I never expected. He was apologizing, something I never thought could be possible. He was apologizing for everything. Every woman, every intentional and unintentional hurt, every time he overlooked me, every time he disregarded me. He began to cry as he asked for my forgiveness. As much as I "felt" for the space he was in, my heart had grown callous in a way that didn't allow his remorse to penetrate. I didn't doubt his apology, but I had become numb after being beaten down for so long. It was difficult to feel the compassion I knew he wanted. I told him I had already forgiven him. I knew he needed to hear it. I hadn't told him before because the forgiveness was for me not him. It was for my Freedom.

Interestingly, when we hung up, I didn't walk away from the conversation feeling like I had finally won. Instead, I cried a deep, cleansing cry. I cried like a person being freed from a crime they didn't commit. I cried releasing another shackle that had been holding me in bondage. I cried tears for our children. I kinda felt like with me the damage had been done and we couldn't really come back from it, but if he could be better for them then that was all that mattered. I would later find out he apologized to them as well. This was yet another moment in my life where God revealed that all those times I cried out to Him from our basement that He had indeed heard me.

Transitions

I read once that a butterfly can take up to 21 day to come out of its cocoon. This is the very reason that you shouldn't help it get out. The wings of this beautiful creature gain strength by beating them against the cocoon. I never did any research to know whether it was true or not, but I likened my life to that of a butterfly. I needed to come out of my cocoon even if my transition was more like years instead of days.

Initially when I left, I thought I was like a butterfly but looking back, I was probably more at the beginning of my transition. I was still beating that cocoon and had only managed to make the layers thinner. Nevertheless, each leg in my journey was important in my growth. Each transition was a learning session from the school of life that is priceless in one's existence. Those first few weeks in my new home were scary and exhilarating. The shower never felt so good and the bacon always tasted great. I took my time in the shower, getting dressed, moving about my day. I began to wash away years of hurt, pain, and uncertainty the best way I knew how. Many mornings I stood in the shower and cried. I cried at what I had done. I had left when he said I never would. I left when he said no one would ever love me. I cried at the joy of being alone without that mess. I cried because I was living the rest of my life differently.

Two weeks after I left him, I decided to get a tattoo of a butterfly. The butterfly represented me. For me, it was the symbol that was a reminder of my courage, my emerging voice, and my journey. It was reflective of my rough start, my crawling around life at the mercy of those around me, my cocoon, and now my emergence. I put the tattoo on my back where I carried all the shit the world threw at me. It was on the back that used to bend under the weights of bags I was made to carry that were never really mine. It was on my back so that *they* could see my wings. *They* are the ones who molested me, hurt me, abused me, ignored me, and counted me out.

I went back for a time. Back where you ask? Back to him. I know, I know! How could I? For years I struggled with getting a divorce. I loved being on my own, but the finality of divorce was difficult to wrap my head around. Every time I would consider starting the paperwork I would pause. Oftentimes I would question myself. *Had I done enough? Did I do all that I could have or should have done? Will God be mad that I am getting this divorce?* This was a real part of my struggle. So, when we decided to try again, I went back understanding if it didn't work, I tried and could walk away knowing I would need to finalize that divorce.

It only lasted a few months. He couldn't fully grasp the woman I'd become, so in small ways he would try and treat me like the woman I used to be. Yet, each day I had to remember who I had become. I had to remember that butterfly. There were a few times I would see the woman I once was trying to resurface but I wasn't having any of that. People questioned why I went back. Those who knew me well knew the reason had to be complicated. Some even went so far to ask what the hell I was doing, but a few just watched from afar and waited. So, when the day came that we both just looked at each other and realized that his changes weren't enough for me and my changes were too much for him, we walked away. He got cold feet for a moment, but I told him it was for the best. We'd been through too much that I didn't have the energy to repair, and I had moved to a place where it didn't really matter because I didn't want it. Deep down, he didn't either. Unlike the first time, there was no deceit in why I was leaving because in a way he left too.

A week after I left the second time, I filed for divorce. I say I left but I never left that apartment, and he didn't give up his place, so it was more about leaving the relationship in its entirety. That time I was ready for real, but I wasn't prepared for the emotions that come with the final judgment. The divorce part, if you must, was easy. He didn't fight it. We didn't need to work out custody or child support because we'd already come to our own agreement. Even when I was in the courtroom with my attorney and the judge said he didn't need to be there, I was fine. However, when the divorce was granted and I walked out that courtroom alone, I felt exposed. I no longer had the option of calling on my "husband" when I needed him. There were no more obligations to one another, no bond, nothing. The shit you feel when this realization hits is another level.

Being on your own is nothing like feeling all alone on your own. As fucked up as our relationship was, there was a covering I felt when I had a husband. When a divorce is granted, you can feel that severing. I mentioned it to another woman I knew, and she confirmed what I felt. There was no preparation for it. It wasn't enough to make me wish I hadn't done it, but it was enough for me to empathize with women who struggled with a divorce once it was final.

The next few weeks felt hard. Emotionally, it took some getting used to, but I'd grown my wings and I needed to fly, my way. So, I started the next leg of my journey as a single mom and a divorcee.

Morning Conversations

She called right on time, but I wasn't quite ready. I'd just woken up. I knew what I wanted to ask her. I knew the direction I wanted her to move in. But she wasn't ready to move there yet. I think when a person goes through trauma and then must relive it to tell the story, it affects them in ways the listener doesn't always understand. So, I expected a residual coating to anything she might say today. I took a sip of my coffee.

"Ok I'm ready." I asked the first question. "When you left the second time, where did you go?

"We dated a bit but that didn't work because my children saw me backslide. I was becoming that woman I used to be, and I had a thought. I can't control the woman he sees but I can control the woman I am. So, I told him. We can't do this. It's not working."

When I heard her answer, I thought she didn't understand what I asked, but as she kept going, I realized she wasn't done with that part. She was still in that space with him. She didn't hear me when I asked, "WHERE did you go?" I took a breath and asked again, "Where did you go after your divorce?" I wasn't sure how she would answer given her first response, but I was sure it wouldn't be what I expected to hear.

She chuckled slightly to herself and said, "This is when the truth about God smacked me in the face. I always thought I had a relationship with my husband up until that point. Then I realized I never had a relationship with my husband. I realized I needed a relationship that could cover me, protect me, and I never really had that. I was in a space where I couldn't depend on anyone, not even me, so I chose God. I decided it would be me and God through thick and thin. Once I made that decision, I was good. I was on solid ground with God. My decisions were better, my steps were better.

Now don't get me wrong, fear and doubt still reared their ugly heads but I had God with me. With God, you can face anything.

She paused. So, I questioned, "What did you do?"

"What do you mean?" she responded.

"Who emerged after your divorce?"

"I want to say the 4-year-old did. But also, the 6-year-old, the 8-year-old, the 16-year-old, the 20-year-old. They all came out. Probably because that's when I was closest to God. It was like a group hug moment; I looked at each of those people inside me and said, 'We did it! We made it.' Then I asked myself why. I looked at each of the girls within me and realized that I am here because they didn't give up on me, so I owe them. So, my life's mission is to now walk in my purpose."

I heard her voice crack and she sniffled. She had another layer opening. I took a sip of coffee and let her finish, careful not to interrupt her flow.

"When I left him, I felt like as much as we weren't together, I still couldn't blossom. I hated that. We started divorce proceedings, but it took some time to finalize. We weren't together but I still called on him in a crunch when something major happened in my life. As messed up as it sounds, I understood why people who are locked up prefer being in the cage of jail. It's predictable. There is no thought to what they must do and like prison, the space with him was predictable. Calling on him when needed was predictable; the arguments were predictable, but I still wanted out of that predictability. A part of me was screaming to get out of the cage I was in and at the same time, a part of me was scared to leave. One minute I was out enjoying my new freedom but when it felt overwhelming, I longed for the cage. Hence, I would put myself back in with each call. This new space, this new life was far from predictable, and it unnerved me."

Then she stopped. It took me a minute to realize she was done but I wanted to be sure. "Anything else you want to talk about?"

"No ma'am. I think I'm good."

And just like that, we hung up.

A Rainy Morning

"Good Morning." I sounded like I had a frog in my throat. I wasn't fully awake, but I needed to be alert.

"Good Morning," she replied.

"You ready?" I was hoping she said no. I was tired. I'd been up at different times of the night all week because my child was sick. I was really hoping the answer would be no, so that we could do this another time. But I was prepared for her to say yes, because a small part of me knew we needed to get this done.

"Yeah...let me get my laptop," Shanice replied.

I had just started making a cup of coffee. Usually, I would be on my second cup, but I slept through my alarm, so I was behind in my coffee time.

"So, let's talk about your growth, your life during the time you were trying to come out of that cocoon. You had wings but they hadn't expanded yet, they couldn't expand, you were still transforming. Like, where were you? Who were you? What did that transformation look like?"

She was quiet for a moment. It was as if she was really trying to grasp what I was asking. Then she took a deep breath and said, "I guess it's a matter of me flexing. I would compare it to someone who keeps their dog in a crate. After the initial feeling of being locked up, the dog finally accepts that it has been released. The dog will move quickly and see all that it can do when it realizes it's out and not going back in the crate. So, when I was out on my own, I enjoyed everything and I started to flex my inner muscles, my inner voice. I was louder than I should have been, my arguments were harsher than they needed to be. I was always on the offense because I wasn't going back to the cage.

During that time, I was learning how to really parent. How to be present with them and others. I can remember hugging my children and really embracing that space and that energy. I was like a college kid who just moved into their dorm room. You know that feeling of being on your own which is both scary and exciting. The energy you feel from that independence that's in everything around you. All of my decisions weren't the best."

She stopped. It was as if she was remembering something or someone that she wasn't yet ready to discuss, and then she said, "The people I may have hurt during that time that I shouldn't have." It was more like a phrase than a complete sentence. She said it so low that I almost didn't catch it. And then we paused and sat in silence for what felt like eternity. Just when I was about to tell her that maybe we should stop for the day, she spoke again.

"I began to look at that ugly ass couch I was sleeping on and realize I needed something better. I spent two years on that couch. It took two years for me to buy a bedroom set. Two years to realize I was an adult, and I was by myself. See, having a bedroom set represented me relinquishing all rights, all molestations that happened in a bed. That couch I kept sleeping on each night had become a security blanket of sorts. I didn't have to be intimate with anyone; I didn't have to be alone. On the couch I didn't feel alone. Having to go to bed alone at night is a sure reminder of whether you are with someone or not. At least that's how it felt to me.

"When my bed arrived it still took another month for me to fully sleep in it. Then one day I felt like it was time. I know it doesn't sound like a big deal but what I felt on the inside was a very big deal. I had just seen a post on social media about a woman who needed a couch because she was going through some things, and just like that I decided to give her my couch. She needed the security of that couch more than I did, so it was going to be hers.

"Once I got my bedroom set and started officially sleeping in my room, I became a bitch. It was so not what I expected but nevertheless it was what I became. I would kick a motherfucker out quick. Even if it meant lying or picking a fight to get it done. Looking back, I know that part was about control. Controlling what happened in that room. Many people said I became like a dude. It was hard to the point where I couldn't even pretend to be soft and pink. For the first time, I could control every aspect of that space. Remember bedrooms were where my nightmare started so to get back that aspect was a huge deal."

"Ok, I've got enough," I interjected. "Let's take a break; you are starting to sound like we are back at the beginning."

She couldn't hear herself, but she was starting to move to a place of anger and not empowerment. I was nervous that she would move back to that space we had already left. She had come so far, been so brave to tell enough of her story to an audience she would never know but I needed her to move through all her spaces. Each one in a careful, deliberate way. One that flowed so people could see that although she went through some shit, she didn't remain stuck in those spaces. She interrupted my thoughts and spoke with a quiet conviction.

"I know...It's like when you go to the gym. When you look at the results you don't think about the sweat, all the push-ups, all the aches, all the work. Doing this is like that for me. I never had to think about what it took for me to get here. Now I'm being asked to remember all of that. You know it's still hard for me to go into my basement because so much of the shit with him before went down in our basement. Different basement, same feelings. I guess it means I still got shit to work on because I didn't even realize it 'til I just said it."

She paused. It was as if she needed me to say something, only I was at a loss for words. How would I know what to say? In all my years, I'd never experienced that level of pain. It's the kind of pain that cuts to the bone. I waited. Just in case she had more to give. I owed it to her to wait. It was my responsibility to let her process all the emotions in her space. When I was sure she was ready for it to be done, I spoke.

"You gon' write today?"

"Umm hmm."

"If you think about our conversation today and have more to give then I think you should write on it."

"Yea, I will."

I wasn't so sure that she would though.

My Growth in Transition

The conversation we had was hard. I woke up a little before 5am and waited before getting on my knees to converse with the One who woke me up. He wasn't finished with me yet. I had work left to do and it was clear that part of that work was the conversation I was going to have with my sister. Even though I woke up before 5am, I laid there for a while. The plan was for her to call at 5 but the time came and went, and my phone was silent. It seemed like I waited forever before drifting back into a comfortable sleep. It was only twelve minutes later when the phone rang. She called to say she needed five minutes and would call me back. I wasn't sure what we were going to discuss but I wasn't up to it. I didn't want to walk down memory lane. I didn't want to relive whatever space was coming. I know her and I knew she'd ask all the right questions. I wanted to stay in bed next to my husband and enjoy that space but as quickly as I had that thought another barrage of thoughts came. *You endured so much so they wouldn't have to. You walked it so you could tell them what not to do. You made it so you could tell them what the other side looks like.*

Now don't get me wrong, I don't believe I am the poster woman for having all the answers to life, nor do I believe that I am some sort of sacrificial lamb. I do believe that we all go through things, and when we do it's not meant for us to hold on to it like a dirty little secret never to be talked about. Odds are what we have gone through, someone else has as well or they will, and we are meant to share our story. Most times we don't share and for me that's a problem because another woman cannot know what the victory looks like if she can't see it for herself. That's where each of us comes in. It's why our stories are important. So, I got up. I got out of the bed I so wanted to stay in, and I got down on my knees to thank God for another day. I praised Him for another opportunity to share my story.

I had just settled in at my kitchen table when she asked me to tell her about my growth. She asked about the time where I felt like I was still in the cocoon and I was strengthening my wings. She wanted to know what that looked like for me. I hadn't thought about that time in a while. It took a minute for me to answer the question. I wasn't expecting her to ask about that so the walk down memory lane was different from the other conversations. I started out thinking, *'Ok my growth...cool. I can talk about that.'* Then I thought more about it, possibly a second too long, and I had to question if I had truly grown.

I was so used to being in that space that I never took the time to think about the transition. I never thought about how the downpour of life that was all consuming eventually shifted to a misty rain and then to sunshine. It was that space of the mist that she was referring to. The space in between the shit storm downpour and the sunshine. That space where I still got wet but not drenched. It's that space where a person can function but can easily get tripped up if they aren't careful. I made many mistakes in that space trying to find my voice and figure me out. Things like what I liked without the influence of another person were truths I had to learn about myself.

Up until this conversation, I'd only told her about the moments that seemed like big moments to me although all of it was an uphill battle; all of it contributed to my growth. I told her about the couch. The shit couch that I'd slept on for years. I'd told her about the freedom that couch represented but I hadn't discussed the memories I wasn't quite ready to let go of. That couch defined me so getting rid of it too soon would've been like someone getting stripped of a title suddenly without notice. You know how you have something so long that when it's taken you feel as if you are suddenly nothing. Good, bad, ugly, or indifferent, that couch gave me something to hold onto until I could figure out who I was and who I wanted to be. I would leave the house each day, ready to find me. I would experience life through new eyes each day, but I could only do it because I knew the "old" me was waiting on that couch and I wasn't ready to let go of her yet. It was my security blanket. I told her about getting my bedroom set, another key move. I hadn't told her that although the moment was powerful, I only rode the wave until fear settled back in. It took a while before I gave that woman my couch. Whenever I made a decision while I was in my emotions, it could go either way. Yet, this decision I was sure of. I made it without the influence of another person and that was what made it the right one. Deciding to get rid of the couch was good but I moved quickly, like my life depended on it. I had realized that holding on to that couch was like working out to the same routine over and over. To get to the next level, something would need to change. I wanted to get to that next level, so I got the bedroom set. Then fear crept in. *You sure you can do this? Don't let her go; she is your constant. You are going to need a living room set. Why would you go out and spend more money you don't have?* Fear is a real piece of work, and she won. I let her stay a little while longer. I guess I let Fear stay too.

These were the moments where my wings were burning. Where the battle between my wings and the cocoon felt equal. I didn't know at that time that I was winning. I didn't realize that although the cocoon wasn't growing, I was in strength. I was getting stronger because I didn't stop moving, I didn't stop trying. Even though I fed into the old me at moments in my life, I gave a greater portion of myself to the new me. Looking back, I thank God that the old me was represented as that big ass couch and not a little trinket because I might have walked around with that in my purse.

It was during that time that the constant loop in my head was, '*C'mon Shanice, you got this.*' Slowly I began to make decisions with more confidence. Something as simple as dinner decisions, the color of my walls, or the outfit I would wear to work all became important. I could feel my wings spread. I would take a shower and release tears that I held for years. I was unapologetic in those tears and I allowed myself to feel all that I needed to. I would have conversations about the lies I ate. I needed to hear them and forgive myself for accepting them. Forgiveness took time because with every lie, I added excuses for the lie and then had to forgive myself for that. I soon began to realize that my forgiveness had to come with no conditions. 'I forgive you as long as...' was not true forgiveness. Forgiveness for myself had to come without a price or a stipulation.

It was in my transition that I began to love me. I began to accept my imperfections perfectly. I realized it was those imperfections that made me strong; it also gave me something to work on. My mornings consisted of seeing myself each day with the expectation of love which meant I needed to wake up every day and rise to the occasion. Loving me meant having my moments with God. It meant taking care of my body. It meant allowing me to feel joy and happiness. It also meant allowing me to feel sadness without it consuming me. It meant learning to dance in the rain. If you took a butterfly and put it back in a cocoon it would die. If a butterfly came out of its cocoon and just sat there never using its wings, it would die. The point is movement is a must for growth. In my case, it meant being honest with myself at whatever cost.

And Then There Was Jackson, but Thank God for Michael

"Hey, you ready?" I ask tentatively.

"Good timing, chick. I had a crazy headache and Marcus just prayed over me and it literally left," she replied softly.

"Ok, you need a few minutes?"

"No, I'm good."

"Ok. Let's start. Alright so Jackson..." I started and then paused. We knew we would be getting to him and his significance in her life.

"Jackson..." she said with a snicker. "It's interesting with Jackson. My relationship with Jackson is something I jumped in to way too soon and I think that's because he showed me that he saw me and remembered me. He told me six months before my birthday that he wanted to take me out for my birthday. Though we didn't speak for a while, a week before the day, he called to confirm that we were still on. Jackson showed me the things I wanted that I never thought I could have. He opened the door, took me out, held my coat, and pulled out my chair. He confirmed what Michael said, 'You shouldn't serve, you should be served.' He showed me that I was truly a Queen. He set the standard for the things I now expect from my husband."

She paused like she was in a deep thought and then she said softly, "Sometimes I sit in my car and think, '*I can't believe I'm making this dude walk around this car and open the door.'* Then I'm like, *'Girl, you're worth it!'* These are the conversations I still have with myself, to remind me that I have a crown."

She paused again, giving me an opportunity to ask who Michael was.

"You said that Michael said, 'You shouldn't serve, you should be served.' Who's Michael?" I asked.

She chuckled more to herself, like she was remembering a moment suspended in time.

"It was the early 90's in the Village—Manhattan. That's where I met Michael. He was the first one who really noticed me. When I met him, I'd just finished high school and up until that point any guy I had been with was me just going through the motions. I was that four-year-old, that six-year-old, that girl that was touched by her "cousins," by the janitor, by anyone who could get away with it. I was a girl who became a young woman that served men for their gratification because I didn't know what real love making was. Hell, I didn't even know what intimacy was until I met Michael.

"Like I said, I was hanging out in the Village with my girlfriend at Uno's grabbing a bite to eat when he walked over to where we were sitting. I saw him when we walked in and sat down, but I didn't think much of it. Anyway, he walked over before he left and gave me a note.

'Hi, my name is Michael. I noticed you when you walked by my table, not because of how you looked but because of the fragrance you were wearing. I hope you don't mind me saying, it smells wonderful on you. I would love to have the opportunity to take you out one day. Give me a call if you get a chance. Enjoy the remainder of your day. Michael'

"I was impressed. I mean my fragrance caught his attention, seriously?! Well, I called him and I'm glad I did because it was one of the most memorable summers. He and I went to the park often to play checkers. You know that's a New York thing. Sometimes we would walk the promenade and just talk. See that's the thing—our conversations were endless. He always made me feel like I mattered. Like he truly wanted to get to know me. So, one afternoon after a game of checkers, it felt perfectly normal to drive back to his place.

"Up until that point, he'd only kissed me on the cheek, so I was comfortable. When we got to his apartment, one thing led to another and like clockwork I became that four-year-old and began to serve. I disconnected and did the things I thought he wanted me to do until he gently grabbed my shoulder and made me stop. What I saw next I had never seen—hurt and confusion in his eyes. He asked me what I was doing, and I told him that I was serving him. At that moment everything went silent. I waited for him to say something, anything because I was confused. Then he began to speak in a very careful and tender way. He told me that I was a Queen and should be served and taken care of, not the other way around. The look in his eyes and the tone of his voice was all love and sincerity. Up until that point I had never felt like a Queen or even a princess for that matter."

She took a moment to gather her thoughts and proceeded to let out the rest of her story, gently like the space her time with Michael represented.

"Michael then began to show me what making love really was. He remained gentle as he touched every part of me. He took his time as he kissed my tears and caressed the very painful essence of who I thought I was. He touched a part of my soul. He touched the part of me that made me look at myself differently. I still struggled after Michael, but that struggle didn't remove the seed he planted. The one that said, 'You are a Queen.' So, after going through all that I did with my ex-husband, when Jackson walked around that car to open the door, I remembered who first showed me all those years ago that I should be served."

She stopped again before moving back to the space we were in. She inhaled before she returned to Jackson.

"But Jackson gave me a run for my money because he had some demons he was fighting that made you feel you were constantly living in the space of, "Damn!" Even knowing that, he was a necessary relationship for me. I had to learn that just because someone gave me something didn't mean I needed to give them something in return. I could have merely accepted his kindness, said 'thank you' and kept it moving. But I gave him me. I gave him my body as payment, which I didn't have to do, which I should not have done. I reverted right back to being the four-year-old."

Another pause.

"I learned a lot though. See I realized that our fights were about my demons fighting his. There were times I would leave him outside my house cussing and screaming because I was like, 'I'm not doing this shit.'"

Then she said to me, "I'm glad that when the relationship didn't work, it didn't mess up our relationship because he was willing to sacrifice everyone for the relationship. You were my family, and he was trying to separate that. He was trying to take my foundation, so I had to go. I think he thought the break-up was about him, but it was really about what he was trying to separate me from. I was determined to never be a woman isolated again, to never walk alone out here again, and I had that with you, sis, so it had to end. But if I had to walk that road with him again I would. I would do some things differently, but I would do it to get here."

"Do you think he knew what love was, in comparison to what you have now?" I inquired.

"I think that's an interesting question and I think he knew his perception of love. I think people love based on how they need to be loved. So, he loved me in that insecure, needy way. He needed me to love him in that, 'I need you to stay close to me, never leave kind of way' and that's not that 'let's win the shit out of this relationship kind of love.' The love he displayed just fed his bleeding wounds. He loved on me the best that he could; it just wasn't what was best for me."

She paused for a moment, as if she was contemplating the weight of what she'd just shared. Then she whispered, "Yeah" more to herself than to me.

"That's what you got?"

"Yeah. It was a necessary relationship, so it was cool. I hope he's better. I pray he's better. I'm not able to check on him to see. I also don't want him to perceive my checking as a door that's being opened. The unfortunate thing from my relationship with Eric was that I learned how to shut the door on relationships and not look back, because I'm not doing that again. That type of letting go is a blessing and a curse because who knows what relationships could've been salvaged. But I can't. I won't."

Silence.

"Nah...Self-preservation is no joke."

More silence.

I broke the silence to bring closure to our conversation.
"Good stuff." I can always tell when she's said her fill, and that was it.
"Yeah, good stuff," she replied. "Lawrence on Friday?"
"Yeah."
"Cool beans."

It's Okay to be a Damsel in Distress

"So, it's interesting, but Jackson taught me what I can ask for as a woman from a man. Lawrence taught me how to be a woman with a man. One day I needed to go to the gas station for air in my tire and Lawrence followed me. When we got there, I opened my door to get out and he walked up and said, 'You know it's ok to be the damsel in distress once in a while.' And with that he closed my door and put the air in my tire. He taught me how to let someone else help me, how to let them take care of things. To the world I was hard but with him it was ok to be soft, pink, and cry. He refused to let me shy away from the woman he saw I could be. I grew up with him; I grew up because of him. He pushed me, and that was awesome. And I love him for that. Now when we talk, he sounds like a mom—"

She slightly giggled before she continued.

"—when he says, 'I'm so proud of the woman you've become.' It was him who talked me off the ledge each time I got on.

"I don't think we would've been good in a relationship though. Together we would have sunk. I think I would've allowed him to get me in the ship even though the ship was taking on water and we would've sunk just as sure as my name is Shanice. We saw too many of the broken pieces we each had, but at the same time, I wouldn't be who I am without him. He showed me how to be a friend. He taught me how to laugh out loud. His friendship left me in awe. To see how he would come to someone's aid with no questions asked made me want that type of friend but to also be that type of friend. He was that dude who truly gave a fuck as a friend without expecting anything in return.

"Once I was sick and I needed meds, so I called him. I never asked him if he had anything to do but he came. He put all the meds on the dresser, kissed me on the forehead and left. He is the standard I now hold people to in friendships because he showed me how it's done. He's my dude and I will always be indebted to him."

"But Lawrence loved you," I said.

"Excuse me?"

She almost seemed annoyed at the statement, but I wanted her to explain it. She needed to explain why it remained a friendship. So many people move into romantic spaces like that, yet she didn't.

"Yes, he loved me because we met at a time when we were bruised and really, really broken, but he loved me, and I loved him. But we weren't doctors. We were both bleeding badly from things in our past and all we could do was give each other Band-Aids for the wounds and teach each other new skills along the way."

She thoughtfully paused as she reminisced on what they had shared.

"But I know he loved me."

"Tell me about when you first met."

"We first met—" She chuckled again. "—because our kids went to the same daycare. One day when I was dropping off my son, I saw this little boy crying. He was crying non-stop and looked over at me like, 'please help me,' so I comforted him. That evening during pick up, I saw him with Lawrence, and I told him his little boy was crying this morning and he let me comfort him. So, I asked, 'Do I look like his mother?' and he laughed. Then I saw him again at a birthday party and it was just him. Then I noticed at all the kids' events there was no mom present, just him. We would have mom conversations and he knew more than most of the moms there.

"A few months went by and I found out he sold insurance, which I needed so we agreed to meet up so he could go over things. While we were there we talked about so many things. We talked about things that happened to us that we hadn't shared with anyone. After that, we had a knowing, a bond. He would see me with my ex and give me a look like,

'You are not alone,' and I would give him a look in return that said, 'You know I got you.'

"Tell me how he made you feel as a woman."

"Ummm...he made me feel cared for. If I ever needed anything he was there. Like with him it was okay to need help. He made me feel I could voice needing help and not feel like I was weak because of it. He made me feel like he saw me even when I didn't want to be seen. It was like I regained the sight I lost. Like he tried to show me everything similar to when a child sees color for the first time. With him I could be all of me, all the time. I remember one time we were watching a movie, *The Italian Job*, and I saw a Mini Cooper and said I wanted to drive one of those. A few weeks later, on our way to the city for an event, he arranged for me to test drive that car. In that moment, I realized that I could never be with anyone else who didn't hear or value my voice. Lawrence saw all of me and my words held value. He created a world for me that I wanted to be in because it was a world where I had no limitations, only complete support. It was all love, never judgment.

"How did you know he would love you forever even if you never chose him?"

"Because I knew the person I became friends with. The beautiful thing about Lawrence is that he could see who you were past the bullshit. He and I could argue and when it was done he'd simply say, 'Ok, you need these groceries. So how about I drop them off and we don't have to say a word.' I knew with Lawrence his love was unconditional. He is that person who I haven't spoken to in months but if I call him, short of him being in another country, he would come. I'd bet my last dollar on that."

Lawrence

This was going to take a minute. I knew that when I got up ready to make the call. I knew before she answered.

"Chick, you ready?" I asked.

"Yes, but we may need to go back and forth a few days on this one. There's a lot I need to unpack."

She paused and took in a breath.

"Ok, let's start," she said.

"The wedding was a critical point. Anyone that knew me then knew that shedding a tear in front of people was so not me. The seamstress had not sewn my future husband's tux and there was no time to order one. I had stepped away from Marcus and the kids when Monique, a friend I had known for over 20 years, was like, 'Suck it up.' But that was not what I needed...and then Lawrence came. He walked over, pulled me further to the side and began to speak. He said, 'Listen, I've seen the love you and Marcus have. The telephonic love, the weather the storm love, a love I've never seen, and you guys can get through this hiccup.' In that moment I looked at Lawrence and I realized something. I realized he loved me past his own selfishness, and I genuinely loved what Lawrence and I shared. He loved me enough to not think about how much he wanted me for himself. He loved me enough to really want who was best for me. Through my tears, he kept speaking. 'Fuck what she did, we got this.' Then he walked me back in there and said to Marcus, 'Let's go find you a suit.'

"The next day, Lawrence and I ended up sitting alone for a minute before I walked down the aisle and that was when he shared with me all that was going on in his own relationship and at the same time letting me know why mine could work. He was the one that sat in my living room when I was waiting for the test results from the lump I found in my breast. He was the one who put his arm around me and said it would be okay. What we have is that unicorn shit. That honest, bare, raw love with no conditions. He was that one person in my life who I truly believed and still feels like it."

She stopped to take in the weight of all that she said. She was deeply loved in that best friend kind of way. She was loved like Cinderella even though he would never be her Prince Charming. She was loved exactly as she was without ever having to change anything in her being. She was loved the way you sit with an old friend on a pier at 80 years old and say, 'Remember that time we...' and all you do is laugh at all the ups and downs life throws your way.

She continued.

"It also doesn't hurt that he's fine as hell. Girl, all the times we laughed while we watched women lose their shit when we'd be chilling. I knew the women he brought around wouldn't last because they never moved past his looks. Oddly enough, each female would always ask him, 'Why aren't you and her together?' He always told them that I was just his girl, his best friend. Everyone else saw our ease but I saw our broken parts and our shit show, and that always brought me down when we were together.

"Where is Lawrence now...emotionally?" I asked.

"Emotionally, he's resigned himself to the fact that he's not going to find the one. He walks hand in hand with his hurt, his pain. He carries a lot of past pain, so he walks with it, he drinks with it, and he parties with it. He knows he could do more, but he doesn't want to because it's like his punishment to himself and that hurts to watch. So even though we don't speak as much, I know the cloud he walks with every day. So, when he calls, we talk 'til we find the sunshine. When my best friend calls or I feel led to check on him, we talk. We discuss the cloud so it doesn't consume him, so he can keep living another day in his search. I'm so proud of his accomplishments but I'm so sad that he won't sit and enjoy those things because he won't let himself."

She paused again. I could hear the heaviness in her breathing. The weight of a friend who carries unspeakable pain is always tough to examine, to acknowledge out loud.

"I don't think he will ever be honest with himself. You know it's interesting that his life as a photographer captures the life of others, but he never captures his life. His pictures are phenomenal but if you look closely at the few that he takes of himself, you can see his cloud just behind the lighting."

"That's probably why he won't take pictures of himself."

"That *is* why. Yes, that's *definitely* why. You know as a photographer you get to hide behind the camera because the focus is never on you. It's the perfect profession for someone who doesn't want to be seen."

After that statement, she paused again. She needed to end it. Knowing her best friend was in pain was painful for her. I let her be still for a while and then I said, "Ok, let me read this and digest it and we'll pick it back up."

"Ok," she softly responded.

Marcus

I called her early. I knew she didn't have much left to say on the matter, but she needed to get the rest out. Talking about a friend's pain can bring its own heartache. I think that's why she jumped into the conversation without any real greeting. She knew what she would say and had already decided to get it off her chest as quickly as possible.

"I can't get into particulars with his pain, but I have moments where I say you can do more but it's a Lawrence and God fix, not a Shanice fix. I can't do it anymore. He must fix it, to fight it the way he knows he can. Part of his pain is part of the punishment he puts on himself. As time passes the pain increases and he just hurts."

Silence.

She takes a minute to breathe. For her, this is heavy. It's a crushing weight that she can't carry for him, nor can she fix it.

"But going through what I have enables me to talk to him and give him a minute to laugh."

"How do you think Marcus felt about Lawrence?"

"He didn't like it. He said I don't want you to meet him to talk about insurance. He didn't vibe with him, so I expressed just enough to Marcus about Lawrence to let him know we were cool. I held back at first because I didn't think he'd understand the nature of the relationship. Marcus and I were long distance so there were things Lawrence could help with as my friend that Marcus couldn't especially because of the distance. So, I explained to Marcus that I didn't want to choose between my friend and my future husband. He didn't make me choose, and because of that I could open up about our relationship. I didn't change my tone when I was on the phone with Lawrence; I didn't hide our conversations. I needed

Marcus to understand that Lawrence was my friend. If I said, 'I love you Lawrence' at the end of a call it's just a friend thing and nothing more.

"By the time we got our engagement pictures from Lawrence, Marcus began to see my relationship with Lawrence differently. He started to understand our connection and not be threatened by it. So, when Lawrence stepped up and helped us at our wedding, Marcus could then say, 'I see why you're friends. I understand why you love him.' It didn't mean Marcus didn't have that small thought in the back of his head that wondered, but we discussed that before, and he learned to trust that it's only a friendship. He learned that when I say I don't cross lines, it's the truth. When I say I value friendships, it's because the few friends I have are as close as family without the blood ties."

Then she stopped. She was finished. As abruptly as she began, she finished the same way. No closing statement. Nothing to wrap things up. It felt like an unfinished story of pain that perhaps could only really be finished by Lawrence, which is why she stopped. Whatever it was, she was ready to move on from Lawrence. She needed to let his pain stay with him. She couldn't carry it, nor could she fix it. She could only stand in the wings and pray for her friend. So, we moved on from Lawrence.

"Hmmm....Marcus gave me what I needed in the very beginning. I met him at a critical point in my marriage. As much as I knew I was leaving that marriage, I was still walking with a lot of lies."

"No one will love you like I do."
"Who's gonna want you."
"You're not good enough."

"I was walking through my life with that view, Eric's view of who I was in my head. So, when I met Marcus I operated from that place. Everything Marcus said was the direct opposite of what Eric said. Our conversations went beyond the superficial, 'I'm too ugly' or 'I'm too skinny.' Our conversations touched on the core of who I was and where I was going. Each conversation was a seed planted that made me say, 'Yes, I can do this.' I met Marcus at a point in my life where I was standing on the ledge ready to jump. And yes, one could argue that I was jumping out of the prison of my marriage and into freedom, but I felt like my ex still had the keys to that freedom. So, I was paralyzed on the ledge, unable to move. Marcus showed me that I was the one with the keys and all I had to do was leap. I had just left when we met and as much as I said to myself that I didn't want a man, Marcus made me realize that I just didn't want *any* man; I wanted the right man.

"Marcus not only planted seeds, but he watered them to ensure they would grow. If I was in a house that was a fixer upper and all I could see was what was broken then Marcus was that person who showed me the beauty in some of those broken pieces. But he didn't stop there. He helped me recognize what to keep because of its value and what to throw away.

"There is a *Seinfeld* episode where Kramer has this itch on his back that needs to be scratched in the worst way but no matter what he did, he was unable to reach his itch because of its location. The only way he could satisfy it was with a back scratcher or the corner of a wall. Kramer ends up meeting a woman with super long nails one day and she notices he is struggling with his itch and offers to help. Much to his surprise, he realized she was serious. After accepting her offer, he was overjoyed to find that her nails were just what he needed. So, she began to scratch, and he was in complete heaven. Day after day, he would meet her, and she would go straight for his back and start to scratch. He loved it, until one day he no longer had an itch. For a while he didn't tell her that he no longer had the itch because he wanted to continue with the relationship. So, he faked until he could no longer take the backscratching. Eventually, he ended things with her because beyond the itch there was no longer a need for her in his life. She kept attempting to cater to a need he no longer had to hang on to the relationship, but neither of them was being fulfilled at that point.

"So, here's my point. Like that story, eventually, I knew that Marcus had to go because I had moved on and grown from that space of need, but Marcus hadn't. I knew what to keep and what to get rid of in my life. I was continuing to grow in my journey, just differently, and he wasn't growing with me. I refused to stay with a person who played lifeguard when I no longer needed that. So, I had to step away because my growth and my life were dependent on it."

Have You Ever Heard a Butterfly Cry?

I Haven't Forgiven Me

The phone rang unexpectedly. It was her on the other end.

"You have a minute?" she asked.

"Yea, I'm just wrapping up some stuff."

I could tell she had something on her mind. I looked at the calendar just to make sure I hadn't missed an appointment with her to "talk." I hadn't. There was nothing scheduled so I picked up my notebook and pen. She was ready to give me something, so I turned off my laptop and prepared to write.

"What's going on?"

She took a deep breath before she began.

"I haven't forgiven me," is how she started, then she moved into that space where she speaks freely without any prompting on my end. "I don't know what that looks like. I know from a Bible study perspective that I'm more capable of forgiving myself, but I still don't know what that really looks like."

Silence.

"I struggle still. My struggle is the woman who watched the other blows my family members endured because I was afraid to move. That woman who stayed was the other me. The me I was before. That woman—she gave what she had, whether it was a Band-Aid given to Symone with the extra-long hug because it was all she had left to give. I struggle with that woman and the woman I am now. So, I need to do this today. I need to talk about this so this will be complete."

I stopped her. "This is raw, chick. Are you sure?"

"This feels very raw and I think it's because it was easier to forgive him than it was to forgive her—me, which is crazy."

"You said you were in the car with Symone having a conversation when these feelings came up. How did you feel explaining your struggle to your kid?"

"I felt surprised because I didn't expect that to come out. I felt like I just walked into an AA meeting and said, 'Hey my name is Shanice, and I am an alcoholic,' because I wasn't aware this unforgiveness was there. Clearly, I hadn't forgiven myself for everything. Then I felt sad because I can't separate myself because we will always be connected. It was easy to pretend I could separate myself from the four-year-old me, the six-year-old me, the other me. But now I realize, shit, they're all me. I battle the part of me that says, 'What if my children say they're dealing with something because I was weak.' And I know I'm not weak, but I felt weak. I'm upset that the stance I take now is not the stance I took then. I'm upset that the fight I have now is not the fight I had then. There-in lies the issue I have with me."

"How do you work to forgive yourself? Like what does the work entail? Do you even know?"

"Nope. I have to believe though that God didn't bring it to light without a plan. These parts of me that still need forgiveness have been dormant in me too long, so it still affects me in ways I wasn't aware of. Maybe I didn't look at all of me as one person because I didn't want all of us to go up in flames."

Pause.

"I need to forgive her, and she needs forgiveness and to be acknowledged for who she was."

"Ok, so when do you want to start having those conversations?"

"About her?"

"Yes."

"I have to have those right away because I am her and she is me and right now we are both at a standstill."

"Ok, let's start tomorrow," I suggested.

"Yea," Shanice said softly. "My perception of her is my ex-husband's words so it's how I still talk to her, how I talk about her, and how I remember her."

Since she kept talking, I assumed she was not finished as I initially thought. "We can keep going today."

"Uh...Nah!"

We both laughed at the way she said it and welcomed the break of feeling the seriousness that unforgiveness of self can create.

"I pretty much told you where I am with that and helping the women that I can. Being on this walk with God has helped me see forgiveness of myself differently, realizing the reasons behind the storms and learning not to condemn myself for how I walked through."

She wasn't really done. She had a little more left still to give. I knew it when I asked her earlier, but I've known her long enough to know how to wait her out until she's ready.

"Before I recognized her, she was just that woman who went through abuse for over ten years. She has earned the right to be acknowledged because she kept me alive. If she didn't have that anchor of faith, I wouldn't be here. I got my strength on her back and now I choose to honor her and thank her."

She spoke of this woman in third voice because she was not ready to fully attach her to herself. On some level I got it. It's hard to see all of you at once and accept those parts on a level where all those parts of you are one. So, I asked her, "How are you going to honor her?"

"You know what? I don't know all the details, but I think it's about how I live the rest of my days. She continued to stand and fight even when it seemed to others she was silent. So, it is a lifelong honor thing."

She paused before simply stating, "But I'm excited. I can tell you that."

Now she was done. She was silent. With her I always know the difference between her being finished and her just taking a pregnant pause—those moments to gather her thoughts instead of the end of her thoughts.

"Ok, this is good stuff. We'll pick back up on something else in a few days."

"Cool beans," Shanice replied.

Have You Ever Heard a Butterfly Cry?

How Do We Function?

'Give me a minute' is what the text said. I responded with an *'ok'* and waited. Today would be different as we would be discussing her current beau. Her new relationship. Today would be different because she would reveal things I'd never heard and never known. There are always aspects of our relationships that we keep to ourselves, only revealing them when it's necessary or the time is right. Today it was necessary, and the time was right.

The phone rang.

"Hey, chick! You ready?" I asked as I normally do.

"Yes."

"So how do you guys function? How do you move...together?"

She jumped right in. No lead in, no intro. She just cut right to the story. I was surprised as usually she gives more by way of a conversation between us before starting but I think she was ready to get this off her chest.

"As much as I love waking up with him each day, I miss the long distance. When we were long distance, we would fall asleep on the computer so we could wake up with each other. We had to get creative with everything from our dinners to movie dates. There was a time when I would wonder what our relationship would be like permanently. See, I tend to get bored with people. With intimacy, I'd shut off so knowing he was coming back I was scared because I didn't know how I would react. Even my daughter said, 'I hope you still like him when he gets here.' So, I told him the challenges he would face with me. I told him I would get bored and there was a strong possibility of me getting cold and distant. I didn't want to get that way and I told him I didn't want to be that person. So, we tried it anyway. I guess he must've been really confident because he came and said he wasn't worried."

She contemplated what she was about to say.

"I still worry a bit that one day I'll wake up and be like, 'Ok, I'm over it,' but I haven't. We laugh about it but it's important. So, I'm better overall with this relationship. He helped me grow and showed me in a lot of ways I needed to grow up some more despite how grown I already was."

"Let's talk about him from a companion angle. How do you function as a team?" I needed to hear how they function. How they move together and apart. She chuckled in a light-hearted loving way.

"I always laugh at that because he is my Steadman. He is my back-up. He is amazing support to the point where it could be a detriment because he will support everything I do. Recently with the Bible studies, I've had to tell him I don't need support; I need him to lead. So, now I see he is amazing at supporting and leading, but he wouldn't have done it if I didn't tell him to do it. I think being in the military has him move in a way where he will give me exactly what I want but I sometimes need him to go outside the box. I feel like the military took the fire out of his creative side which he is now trying to get back. He is that guy who is mindful so I'm careful to sometimes ask him if he has too much on his plate because I want him to feel appreciated."

She laughed in a way that told that she's enamored with him.

"It's great. And where he falls short, I'm ok with it. You must be ready to accept that a person may not reach the potential you see. But the patterns he has, I'm willing to spend the rest of my life with. Happily."

She was done. There was finality in the way she said 'happily' that let me know. It was almost like *happily ever after, the end.* That was short and sweet, but I had what I needed.

"That was good," I stated. "I'm going to look at this tonight and examine where we move from here."

"Alright, hon."

"And then I'll reach out to you."

My Best Friend

Her questions were hard. It wasn't always clear as to what she was asking and sometimes I just wasn't ready to answer it. I needed a minute to put it into my words. I needed a minute to wrap my head around it so I could feel it first, then answer. It felt like it was much harder than it should be...but why? This was my husband. I'd married my best friend. She knew this. She knew how we met, how our relationship evolved, the back and forth, the ones in between. She knew me. Each time we spoke recently I could tell she was searching for more, but she did things in the way she always does. She pressed me but not to the point where it seemed like she was leading me.

Recently she'd asked me how we function, and I swear I had no clue what she meant. I gave her what I thought she wanted but as I kept rolling the question around in my head, I knew I didn't even give her half of what I felt. What I felt and what I told her just wasn't the same. So, a few days later, after we were just catching up on each other's lives, I asked her, "What did you mean when you asked me how we function?" Her answer came so fast and seemed so simple it made me wonder if I even heard her correctly the first time. But she worded it differently, so I knew this time she made it crystal clear in a way where I got exactly what was being asked of me.

"Well, when I asked how you functioned, I wanted to know how the two of you move as a team. This place where you finish each other's sentences wasn't always the case. So, how did you get here because he's your bestie beyond me."

It made perfect sense. But instead of having yet another conversation, I just asked her if I could write it down and send it over because I could think about how I wanted my emotions to come out. I could make sure I didn't miss anything. I could speak from my heart after I digested all of what I had to say.

I knew how we moved. How we functioned. How we got to the place where we finish each other's sentences. All of it is like breathing for me. It often feels effortless, like we were meant to be here, like we were never meant to function without one another. To breathe, I need my lungs, and I need my body to house those lungs. So, the team of he and I and its success is contingent upon it being he and I. To say he gets me is an understatement. He took the time to really know me and I appreciated that. He took the time to get to know the me he wanted to be friends with and not the me he wanted to marry. He took the time to know the me he wanted to see be and do better, the woman I was still evolving into. It's apparent in the way we flow that we studied each other, but more importantly, we took the time to study ourselves to ensure our movements were in sync.

It was a time of growing pains, missteps, unnecessary arguments where he had to remind me that he wasn't 'him' and my argument was misdirected. If it was anyone but him telling me that, I'd go off, but the love that lingered behind his eyes told me that although he was seeing the worst parts of me he was still there. It was what was behind that look that forced me to listen. It was when I stopped that I realized he was that man that was loving me back to health and a better me. He didn't tell me to cut the crap. Conversely, he said, "I will sit in the shit with you but don't flip out on me when we are sitting in the shit that belongs to you and all I want to do is ensure you don't sink while figuring it out." He showed me on more occasions than I can count that he was always in my corner and not because of the big picture of what could be. He was in it for the here and now despite what that big picture might look like. That told me that if our hopes and dreams never materialized, he would still be there.

How could I not love someone like that? How could I not rock with someone like that? He looked beyond my exterior and saw my heart. He looked beyond my pain and saw my joy in waiting. He looked beyond my fight and saw my fear. The more he looked the less I fought. The more he talked, the more I listened. The more he listened the more I talked. The more he protected me, the more the walls that I built to protect myself fell. He didn't feel the need to fix me; rather he walked with me as I figured out what my healing looked like.

We both had some healing before getting together, but to heal separately and then heal as a unit are two very different things. Separate healing is just that, separate. But healing together comes with its own challenges. We had to be patient while tempering our own expectations. We had to acknowledge that this wasn't a race and if one took longer than the other, we shouldn't gloat but encourage. We had to ensure that we didn't need to be in a space of who knows more than the other. Rather it had to be about what we could learn together about ourselves in this space with each other.

We live in a space of love and safety. Safety was big for me. There was a point that I didn't need anyone to *love* me, I needed to feel safe with them. With him I feel safe. With him I know my heart is protected. With him I know my beliefs, my life, my words, my fears, all of me is safe. I would go to the ends of the earth for him because I know that if I was to ask him, he would do it for me. But honestly, I wouldn't have to ask because he would already be there.

So, I sent to her in an email, all my thoughts about how we function. A few hours later I received a text from her asking, 'When did you realize that your friend was your bestie and that you loved the friendship so much more than the possibility of a relationship?' I guess she hadn't read the email yet. Or maybe she did but needed an answer to for other reasons. Either way I was happy to answer her.

I knew our friendship meant so much more when I wanted to help him clean up his 'mess' even if it meant making a clearing for someone else. See there came a point where my desires, hopes and dreams for him surpassed my own selfish reasons that would have included me. Him being better was no longer driven by my own relationship agenda. There came a point in time where I knew I could survive the loss of a 'relationship' with him but the thought of losing the friend I had in him shook me to my core. He had become that one that I could share everything with, without fear of any judgment and what it could do to the possibility of any romantic relationship between us. The day I could honestly admit to myself that I wasn't the woman for him because of who I was at that time wasn't what he deserved or needed, created a shift in my thinking. It created a space where I knew that as much as I loved him, I knew his love for me wasn't contingent on a relationship; it was built on the possibility of a friendship. Being able to clearly see that, I knew that I loved my friend so much more than the person who could possibly be my boyfriend or husband. That was the point where I changed how I moved.

My motivation, my direction all began to shift and when I interacted with him it came from a place of just being friends. To do this, I made sure I wasn't putting relationship stuff on him. No pressure, no expectations. I had a good friend, and I would never give him unnecessary girlfriend crap; I knew what my girlfriend crap could look like and he didn't deserve it. There was no space in my head for him to *have* to call me. He didn't *have* to check in. I never asked any other friend to do these things, so I didn't do it with him. If I was legit in helping him clean his mess, then the last thing he needed was pressure from me, his bestie. There were no more girlfriend undertones with what I gave as his bestie. It was just me simply being a reliable friend the way I am with others.

This stance strengthened and solidified our friendship. We still move from this space. I believe it is from this space that we are such a strong couple. Even now I don't give him unnecessary bullshit or attitude because I wouldn't do it with my friends. This space allows me to not get in my feelings too soon. It allows me to see him and not just my emotions on issues. It allows me to hear him and not the voices in my head that try to steer me in another direction. Being best friends allowed me to be me unashamed, unhindered, completely bare, confident in my flaws, and honest about my fears. Being best friends helps us get through each day regardless of what it looks like. Once I realized the true cost of losing that, I knew we were so much bigger than the picture we had in our heads of what a relationship looked like.

I sent that response in another email. A short while later I received a text with a heart emoji. I knew then that I'd given her exactly what she needed. I also knew that I touched a piece of her heart with my response. She knows how I move with a person I consider my bestie, and with that I was done for the night.

Circle of Sisters

I felt His presence in my soul. My spirit whispered that it was time for me to write again. It was time to get some things on paper that I could never—would never say in our conversations. I opened my eyes and got up. I moved to my space. It was the space where my thoughts were uninterrupted. The space where my peace remained. Pen to paper. That's all that was required.

Someone once asked me how I got where I am. They asked how I ended up this way. That question made me look at all I'd encountered along the way. The men in my life, from my father, father figures, uncles, cousins, boyfriends, and friends. Then, I thought about my aunts, half-sister, the sisters who were of no blood relation but stood by me when I felt like my world was falling apart. I thought about their cousins who became my cousins, their friends who became my friends. All the ones who stood in the gap for me when I didn't know it. I thought about my blessings, my grandma who laid down more prayers for me than I can count and our family. So, when I sit in this space of clarity, this space when the smoke and fire isn't blocking my view, I see my sisters standing there cheering me on, carrying my crap, and walking beside me. Each one played a different role in my life, but they were all there. Some were cheerleaders, others were confidants, some were 'yes' women, some were devil advocates, and a few were low key haters, but they all served a purpose. They all were integral in who I am today. I took a piece from each woman, each encounter whether I took it willingly or received things from them that I didn't ask for. Regardless of how I came to acquire those pieces, I look in the mirror each day and see all of them, and I thank God for them because they served a purpose.

I used to spend years hearing about this sisterhood that women experienced. I even watched the sisterhood in all its splendor on the big screen where big moments called for a collective coming together, but I never thought I would experience it or be present enough to realize when it happened. Remember, I was the chick that was always disconnected, always 100 miles away, so even when my body was present my mind was always far away. Then one day it hit me. I had a circle of sisters, walking with me through the various stages of my life that brought me to the place that I stand now.

It was months before my wedding, and I hadn't planned a thing. I'm just not that girl. To be honest I was fine just showing up and looking pretty. Anyone who knows me, knows that I have moments where I will plan and moments I may—possibly on a really good day when all stars are aligned—decorate, but I don't have the zeal it takes to plan an entire wedding. Besides, it was wedding number two and the actual marriage was more important to me than the wedding. Furthermore, planning a wedding sounded like straight work that I didn't want to be a part of.

One day while at work, I mentioned that I was getting married to an acquaintance who is now a close friend. She asked me all the expected questions: *When is the date? What are your colors? Did you get your dress? Where are you going on your honeymoon?* And so many more questions. I didn't mind the questions; it was the fact that I had no answers, and I shrugged so much it was beginning to look like I was doing the Bankhead Bounce. The look on her face made me chuckle, so I started to explain to her that I'm just not *that girl*. Much to her surprise, I stated that I didn't want to plan my wedding which seemed normal enough, but then I said that I didn't want to do a taste testing, venue walk-through, and I didn't want to find a place for the honeymoon. After hearing all of what I didn't want to do, she said, "I'll plan your wedding." I laughed when she said it. *I mean didn't she just hear what I said?* So, I steered the conversation towards work stuff. Not to mention that we'd only just met at work because we were on a committee together and we were at an event, so she couldn't have been serious.

Weeks had gone by and when I saw her again, she mentioned the wedding planning again. So, I had to stop her and say, "Wait, you were serious." It wasn't really a question but more a statement showing my confusion. She responded with a *yes*, so my confusion shifted to shocked and giddiness. We had just met, and she was willing to plan my wedding. What luck! All I had to do was tell her my favorite colors. Then there's one other requirement—it had to be a beach wedding. Everything else she would figure out. All I had to do was wait for her to tell me where to be when the time came. She stated that if she needed any more information, she would contact my husband or my children. Once I didn't have to plan anything, I was excited about what I didn't have to do and what she would come up with.

Another sister friend of mine decided to tackle the reception and honeymoon festivities once she heard someone was planning the actual ceremony. This sister friend said she would handle the transportation to and from the wedding as well as the festivities leading up to my beach wedding. My wedding was being done in two parts. I would have the first ceremony in my hometown and the beach wedding I always wanted would happen days later in Miami along with the reception. After the first ceremony, the plan was that we would all make a beeline to the airport and be on the next flight smoking with family and friends joining us for the beach ceremony and celebration. It was perfect. I would be surrounded by those I love the most for a few days and when everyone left, he and I would remain for our honeymoon.

As the days progressed, Monica would place calls to my children and husband asking for insight on some of my likes and dislikes. She would call after tastings and share her thoughts and menu decisions as well as the cake choices she was making. It was perfect and all that was left was for me to find a dress. One day while at work, a co-worker who I was building a friendship with asked me what kind of dress I was getting. I shrugged. I had no idea. I started to explain that I'd begun looking online to see who could get one to me the fastest. The look of horror on her face as I explained was enough to make me pause.

"What do you mean online?" she asked me.

"I mean I am ordering a dress online and..."

Before I could finish, I heard her say, "Oh God, please tell me you're joking." She was so bothered by this that I laughed to myself. I really didn't understand what the big deal was. It was a dress. A dress I would wear one day. It just wasn't that big of a deal. Yet she insisted on trying to convince me that ordering my dress online would be a travesty and that I should reconsider. I finally gave in and decided I would go to David's Bridal to find a dress. I didn't feel it was necessary, but I figured it couldn't hurt and although it wasn't as cost effective as finding something online, I could still probably find something that wasn't too expensive.

So, we went to David's Bridal. It was my daughter, my friend Vanessa who was planning the festivities after the ceremony, along with the friend who balked at me for wanting to order a dress online. My mom and another friend who I'd known over 18 years accompanied us as well. Two of my friends who couldn't attend in person experienced the moment with us via phone. As soon as I got to the store, I scurried straight to the sales rack searching for anything that was my size. My friends decided that I was not up for the task, so they started their own search for the perfect dress. It was comical to see the reaction on their faces every time I said I found the *one*. They would just shake their heads and walk away as though my efforts were hopeless compared to their search! I wasn't offended, as it was apparent that I wasn't taking it seriously anyway. They came to me with dresses they selected and as I began to try each one on, a feeling inside of me began to awaken. I looked at myself in each dress and realized I looked beautiful.

After the years of shitstorms, unhappy endings, and loss after loss of settling, the idea of a happy ending, of having a fairytale, began to look different. When I stood and looked at myself and realized what I was about to do and who I was going on this journey with, I realized it was possible for me. I thought that me not wanting these things was just that. When in reality it was just me believing I wasn't deserving of these things. I never planned on tasting cakes, picking menus, or finding a dress. It just wasn't what I envisioned for myself but while sitting with friends and family fussing and gushing at each dress I tried on with tears in their eyes, it dawned on me that I deserved this, and when I finally tried on the *one* I knew I deserved all of it. I deserved the life I wanted. I deserved the cake, the honeymoon, the man, and the dress. After friends stopped screaming, high fiving, and hugging me, I decided I wanted that dress.

When I got back to the dressing room, I allowed myself a moment to admire the dress and visualize myself walking down the aisle until I noticed something that made me stop...the price tag. *One thousand dollars! WTF!* No way was I paying that. *Welp, there goes that.* I left out the dressing room and handed the dress back to the sales rep and told my friends we had to find another. They looked at me in shock and asked why, so I told them the price and explained that I couldn't do what I couldn't do so we would have to find another dress.

Vanessa looked at me and asked, "How does that dress make you feel? Does it make you feel as beautiful as you looked?" I told her that it did. Then she said something I will never forget.

"I am going to buy you the dress."

"What?! You can't do that! That's way too much money. It's fine. I can find another."

She refused to listen and paid for the dress. She was someone I'd known less than a year. Don't get me wrong, in our short period of time we walked one heck of a journey together, so I knew that time was just one piece of our friendship. But that moment showed me a lot about friendships. I have never been one to think someone *owed* me for being friends or needed to be loyal because we were shoulder to shoulder in tears. So, with all that we shared through our life stories and work experiences, she owed me nothing but was giving me everything that day by making a dream become a reality. She bought my dress and to this day she still doesn't speak of it. She doesn't tell anyone so they can praise her; she just walks as though this was something everyone does in life.

I was told the plans for the wedding were coming along great. Tickets were purchased, menus planned, rooms reserved, and my dress was altered. So, when the day of the wedding rehearsal came, I was ready. I went to the nail salon with a friend and picked up things I needed for my flight and the honeymoon. When we finished, we went to the church. I was excited to get there. I hadn't seen my soon to be husband since that morning and we hadn't spoken all day. I was excited to rehearse our upcoming moment. I was excited that our moment had come. I couldn't wait, so when we pulled into the church lot I noticed his car right away. We pulled up next to him and I rolled down the window beaming. I expected him to turn to look at me, so when he didn't I knew something was wrong. He just kept looking straight ahead, at the building, with no expression. When I looked a little closer, I realized he was angry. I got out of the car to find out what was wrong. My mind was racing at 100 miles per hour trying to figure out if I had done something to upset him. When I got to his window, he rolled down the window and slowly turned his head towards me.

"What's wrong, babe?" I asked, trying not to freak out. What he said next hit me like a ton of bricks.

"Nothing is done for the wedding."

I was confused at that moment. What the hell did he mean nothing was done? I spoke to Monica, everything was done and paid for but then he went on to explain. It wasn't the parts Monica was handling. It was the festivities, the deejay, the transportation to and from the wedding, the Miami festivities etc. I started to speak but he held up his hand and said there's more.

"My tux is not done. It was never made, paid for, nothing. So, I have no tux for the wedding."

At that moment everything stopped. Not having all the other things hurt but him not having a tux cut deep. I was furious. She was supposed to be my friend and she left us hanging with half a wedding. So many times, I told her she didn't have to do it. She didn't have to plan so much. So many times, I offered to pay, and she wouldn't take my money. I put the money in her hand, she gave it back. She'd made an entire day of taking him to get his tux. To pick it out, get fitted, and in the end it was straight bullshit. All those conversations when she told me about the calls she had made and things she had planned were all lies from the beginning.

With the help of Lawrence, I got past the pain long enough to get through the rehearsal and the wedding ended up being a huge success. Monica worked her magic and got us a local deejay who needed to record some things for his marketing campaign, so we got some things thrown in for free. The transportation was worked out, and the other festivities we figured we didn't need because we were with family and time spent with them would be even better without all the bells and whistles.

After the wedding, I found out everything that my circle of sisters were going to do to make that day great. They had planned to cash in their tickets to get me transportation. See, they already knew about the ball drop before I did, so they started working on all the contingency plans days before. They never mentioned it because they didn't want me to sit in the stress and anxiety days before the wedding; instead, they took on the stress for me. They spent days worrying, crying, cussing, and picking up broken pieces so I wouldn't have to. They knew the road I'd walked to get there, and they were determined not to let anyone ruin it for me. That weekend they revealed their strength in the way they carried my load on top of their own. They showed their love by carrying me when I thought I would fall apart. They showed me their joy by cheering so loudly that I began to cheer to myself. That day, that weekend, I saw their tears of joy and felt their readiness just in case the one that almost destroyed my day suddenly popped up. Oh yes, I am sure if I searched their suitcases I would have found Vaseline and sneakers for the ready if anything popped off! That weekend I realized that my sisters would ride with me to the ends of the earth even if the wheels fell off. That is what the circle does; they close ranks, protect and take care of each other.

Have You Ever Heard a Butterfly Cry?

119

In Sickness & Health

Finally, lots of sex, date nights, and life together, right? Wrong! Our honeymoon was amazing; don't get me wrong. It was my first vacation with someone I was in a relationship with and I loved every minute of it. For years, I never thought I could "tolerate" someone long enough to actually vacation with them. That's why I lived for lunch hours. That's about how much tolerance I had for most people. I just always thought that to go somewhere of any significant distance meant I was *stuck* with them, so vacationing was never an option.

This was different though. We spent days by the pool often speaking, but sometimes just being. This was comfortable, no pressure. I married the right one. This was the happily ever after I'd dreamt about that I never thought I'd have. From the time I put on that wedding dress and began to watch my "never ever after" actually materialize into my "ever after" right before my eyes, I knew I made the right choice, and I was present for every moment. I was on cloud nine and this seemed like the icing on the cake. My previous marriage came with expectations, defined roles, and words spoken and unspoken that seemed etched in stone, but this was different. When we returned home from our honeymoon as husband and wife without those extras, I knew I was different. The first year of marriage was nothing like the stories you hear of painful adjustments while learning to grow together. It was the opposite. It was easy so I didn't fear anything in the future of our marriage...or so I thought.

I remember that day like it was yesterday, that moment like it was a few minutes ago.

"Hey, sweetie." I answered my phone expecting to hear my honey, only it wasn't him.

"Hello. Your husband was in a car accident," said the unfamiliar voice.

It took a few seconds to register. And then it became clear. He was in a car accident. Panic swept over me, a gripping fear that made everything around me seem like it came to a grinding halt. Then I heard her say, "He's ok," as if that was all the reassurance I needed. *Who is this? How does she know? Where is he?*

Then he got on the phone and said, "I'm ok babe, someone hit me."

I heard the pain in his voice. He didn't want me to hear it, but I heard it anyway. I was driving but it felt more like I was being driven in that moment because I had lost all control. I thought I knew our future, but in that moment, I realized how much I didn't know and couldn't control. We talked a few minutes more. He told me the accident happened in front of our home and that he thought his wrist was broken. He said he was waiting for the ambulance. I knew what hospital they'd take him to, but I was hoping to get home soon enough that I could ride with him. I fought back the flood of tears that threatened to fall and drove as fast and as carefully as I could, if that makes any sense. When I got near my house, I could see his car. It looked like Thor took his hammer to it as part of the back end was pushed up to the front seat. The front of the car looked like an accordion. It was a disaster, like something in a movie. I jumped out of my car and walked over to him before the ambulance doors closed. I kissed him, told him I loved him, and would see him at the hospital. I then walked over to the car and cleared out what I could from what appeared to be a mangled mess before it was towed.

When I arrived at the hospital, I was told that he had a broken wrist and back injuries. Both required surgeries. One was scheduled for the next day, the other would be two weeks later. They released him that night and we went back for the first surgery first thing in the morning. Anyone who ever had surgery knows that the times they give you are more like "cable guy times." We were scheduled at 8:30am but we were hoping to be in surgery by 11 am. Eleven o' clock came and went, and the pain was unbearable for him. They hadn't given him anything the night before for pain so at that point I could see his own silent tears fall. I was enraged and was just about to lose it when a doctor walked by and realized what was happening to him. That doctor made a call asking for a "blocker" which was the answer to my anger and his pain.

In sickness and in health... We often say it without considering all that it could really mean. I know when I said it my thoughts settled on sickness being way down the line. Like old age down the line. Certainly not now, but here it was testing and stretching in ways I could have never imagined.

"You need anything, babe?"

"Yea a new back and wrist," he joked.

"What time is your therapy so I can take you?"

"3 pm."

"I got your prescription, babe."

"Thank you, honey."

"Let me get that, babe. It's ok, lean on me. I can take your weight."

That was us. Our new normal, everyday, all day. I was running on five hours of sleep at the most. He was running on pain and pain killers. I would hear him nightly and each night I would ask if he was ok. I wasn't frustrated; I never focused on the "why me" aspect. I just resigned myself to the fact that *our sickness* was here and if the tables were turned he would willingly and patiently do all the things I did for him. We had a foundation that was strong enough to withstand this period and for that I was grateful. God gave me strength and comfort when I needed it. Over time, I came to realize that my "superman," although super, was just a man who could get hurt and feel pain. It was in that space of still recognizing how super he was and how good God still is that I realized we were learning a different level of trust. It was there that I learned that I could trust someone completely to protect my heart, but it didn't mean that we could protect their physical body. So, I embraced every opportunity to be with him as a gift and I reminded him daily that no matter what this looked like at the end, the picture would always be me and him.

He trusted me with every aspect of him and I loved that. That level of trust helped us become stronger together. I helped him put on socks and he would ask how I was feeling. I would ask if he got rest and he would ask about my day. Rather than syncing bank accounts, we were synching schedules for doctor appointments and therapy. Rather than focusing on bills and budgets, we focused on prescriptions and meal plans. There were no extravagant dinners for date night; instead, there were expensive trays so we could enjoy meals in bed watching movies on demand. There were no leisure drives; instead, there were urgent drives to the hospital for pain management or unexpected challenges we weren't equipped to handle. We had to see our sunshine in the rain and make decisions either way. Days I couldn't "fix" him I prayed, nights I couldn't sleep I prayed. Each day was new and brought new things, but I remained grateful because I could've been a widow. I could have lost my best friend. This was marriage; this was us, authentic and unapologetic. This was our love in its most organic state. We listened to each other with the intention of hearing, we loved each other with the intention of loving, and we saw each other with the intention of seeing. This was our house being built. The frame that goes on the foundation.

"By wisdom a house a built, and through understanding it is established; through knowledge its rooms are filled with rare and beautiful treasures." Proverbs 24:3-4

Our Life

Our life slowly made its way back to our "normal." His physical therapy sessions began to slow, his movements were less constricted, and his smile came from inner joy instead of a way to cover up pain. It was in that space that I began to figure out who I was becoming as a wife. This time around I wasn't walking on eggshells, I didn't have to shout to be heard, and I was able to walk within our team my way. I had another person to consider but I knew I was always being considered when decisions were made.

That space, that growth was what I needed. Yet something was still missing and over time I knew what it was. It was God. It seemed so simple that He should be a part of everything, but it was all too easy to move through my days and nights and not consider how the One who created us should be a part of our decisions and our movements. See, I grew up knowing of God, but I'd never really taken the time to cultivate a relationship with Him, not the way I do now. In my darker times I talked to Him, I prayed to Him, I "knew" Him, but I still didn't consider Him in everything I did. I didn't ask if I was supposed to marry this man. I just married him and expected God to bless my union. I don't think many of us ask God about decisions like that. Not because we're trying to avoid an answer. I think it's more because we only include God when we are dealing with something that seems insurmountable. There's a saying: "It's better to ask for permission rather than forgiveness." So, praise God that He's still in the business of forgiveness!

In that space, I began to go to Him with everything, both big and small. I needed a guide and who better to help me find me than the One who created me. During that time, my prayers changed, I talked less and listened more. I waited to hear from Him before I moved. I began to talk to God as much as I talked to my husband. As my relationship with God grew, my relationships with everyone else also grew. Some grew closer while others grew apart. During my growth, I realized my home was out of order. I led our home with so many things but that wasn't quite right. My husband was supposed to not only be my partner, but he was supposed to lead. We were equally yoked, but we didn't move that way. We had many discussions of our love for the Lord, so I knew he prayed but the conversation I needed to have with him was about where God stood in our relationship, in our marriage. We had recently started having Bible study together each night before bed so one night I decided to broach the subject.

"Babe, you have a minute," I affectionately asked.

"Yea, wassup?"

"You know I've been working on my relationship with God, and I love that we read the Bible together; but I need you to be the head of this family."

He quickly answered, "I am."

"No, you don't understand what I mean. I need you to lead us as God says. You need to cover us. I need you to lead."

The covering that I was asking him for was huge. My husband once told me, as a woman you should trust the God in the man so now I was letting him know I trusted the God in him. I was finally in that place.

"Can you do that babe? Can you lead us?" I asked.

We prayed together and read from different places. I found comfort in standing with him as he prayed for us, for our family. Something shifted for us that night kneeling side by side in the presence of the Lord with him as the lead. That moment began our new life. The injury, the therapy, all those things helped us shed our old way of doing things. That moment we became the unit we weren't before, the one with God, my husband, me, and our children. The Bible says that love never fails and with God as the head of our family, we won't ever fail.

Last Talk

It was going to be our last conversation about all she needed to be put on paper. We had so many discussions over the past year that it seemed fitting to get to a point where she could openly discuss "her life." She wasn't the four-year-old trapped in a grown woman's body. She was now a woman whose age matched her grown woman status. She no longer hid her scars and experiences, instead she opened them up to the world, so they transformed from scars to wings, from experiences to journeys. I was excited for this day. It meant she could close this part, something I know she's wanted for quite some time. So, I waited for her to pick up the phone.

"Let's talk about this section of 'Our Life,'" I started. "You're praying together as a couple. He's leading the family; he is the head. It's everything you wanted. You've grown individually and together. He's healing but you're healing too. So, what do you guys have in your future?"

She took a breath before answering. "I don't know what's in our future. I don't really have a picture of our future."

"Ok, well what are we doing about Shanice's picture?" I was essentially asking the same question but a different way. I wasn't sure why she had no picture of her future. I mean, doesn't everyone have a picture of the future? Doesn't everyone have a vision? Maybe I was just asking the question in a way that wasn't clicking.

"Our future looks like the house that houses the family. Our parents don't have to worry where they'll live. Our future will be happy, not happier." She paused as if thoughtfully constructing her next sentences. "The happiness that I have now I plan to carry into our future. I'd like more money, but more money makes things more convenient, it doesn't make us happier. I've always spent so much time running from the present that I've learned to be present in the now. So, as much as I'm planning, I am learning how to enjoy right now. My life is kingdom driven so my future would be that."

I was confused. I knew what a kingdom driven life for God looked like, but she wasn't telling me what her future looked like. She wasn't clear, so I probed further, "What does a kingdom driven life look like?"

Silence.

"Hmm, so I don't have a picture of what a future kingdom driven picture could look like. I have a loosely drawn picture of what I'd like, but here's my issue with that. Sometimes our picture can be so permanent that if God tells us to go left, we don't because it doesn't look like what we imagined it would. Do I hope the podcast and the books do well? Absolutely! But I don't want to be so focused on my picture that I don't see His. I've spent a lot of time listening to God and less time telling Him what I want."

"So, He's given you no picture? He's shown you nothing?"

"I've learned that every picture He's given me isn't one that needs to be shared with the world and every picture isn't always given in its entirety. Sometimes He gives me parts. Recently He's shared what my struggle means. My space of struggle, my hamster on the wheel struggle resembled 1st Peter, chapter 1 verse 7. *'These have come so that the proven genuineness of your faith-of greater worth than gold, which perishes even though refined by fire-of greater worth than gold, which perishes even though refined by fire- may result in praise, glory and honor when Jesus Christ is revealed.'* It is a test. When you have relationships with people who disappoint you and you meet the right one, you often put them through a test. I have never walked this close to God. I mean I've been there but not this committed. So, like the lover who finally has that girl's attention, when he is finished with the test she puts him through, he will say, 'Wow, that was worth it!' That's me right now. I don't need to see the full picture because I know in the end it will be worth it."

But she still wasn't giving me "the picture." She was explaining where she is and how she got there but she wasn't showing me where she was going, where they were going. Maybe they didn't know and if it turned out to be her unknowing, then I would have to be ok with that.

"You mentioned a podcast. What will that entail?" I was trying a different tactic by asking another way.

"Marcus and I will talk about relationship, not religion. We will talk about what it is to have a relationship with Christ. What that could look like."

"And what have you learned about relationship?"

"I've learned that having a relationship with God is like having one with people. There is a time to talk and a time to listen. We must cultivate it. If we don't, how will we know what the other person wants and needs?"

"Ok let's stop. I need this to be recorded." She was opening up. I wasn't sure how I knew but I did. It was here that she would give me a glimpse of what her future looked like, what it was going to be with God at the center of her relationship with her husband. They were embarking on this together and this was her picture, her future. I hit record and we picked up where she left off.

"Ok, so..." I prompted her to begin again.

"Yes, we have to cultivate it. If we don't cultivate it, how do we know what the other person wants and needs, and...and..."

She sighed.

"How can the other person know what we want or what we need. Relationships teach you about yourself. You know my relationship with Christ taught me so much about me. It taught me so much about what I am and what I am not."

She paused and let out another sigh. Each sigh seemed to be like a small release.

"Being able to have this relationship has given me a level of comfort I never had before. I used to go to Him reluctant and worried, but now that I spend time with Him, I realize I didn't have to feel that way. I can go to him with any and everything. And now I look forward to the times where I just pause and listen, sit at His feet, and feel a peace that I could never explain because I don't understand it. You know it's—it's something that I was never taught. I was never taught that I should have a relationship with Him, so I didn't know I could. I looked at everyone else's relationship with

Him and my perception of their relationship with Him was whatever they showed me.

"You know it's not a relationship if someone goes, 'There's Shanice over there. Let me tell you what she's like.' That doesn't mean I'm going to be that for them. It means that's what I am for the person who knows me. Now when I look at someone's relationship with Christ, I go, 'Great, that's what He's done for them!' Although I'm overjoyed for what He's done for them, I want to know what He's going to do for me. He may be a husband to the husbandless, but I've got a husband so what will He be for me? Only when I spend time with Him do I find that out. Only when I sit in His presence do I find out how much He has for me and it makes me realize how much more time I wanna spend with me. You know, my fear was what is He gonna tell me about me? What is He gonna show me about me?

"It's such an exciting space to be in. It's like the relationship you have with someone when you can't wait to get on the phone with them, to hang out with them, or to just be with them. That's what this relationship is like."

Pause.

"It's craaaazy, chick. It's crazy and I'm...I'm...that's why the podcast has to be done."

She stumbled over her words in her excitement, but in that excitement, I learned why the podcast was so special. This podcast was part of her future, their future. I began to see the picture.

She continued.

"I need people to understand you NEED TO HAVE A RELATIONSHIP LIKE THIS! We have relationships with people we can't call at two in the morning, but I can call Him. We have relationships where we can't say, 'Yo, I need this' because they may not give it. They may be selfish, stingy or there could be other reasons, but Christ is none of that. He's always gonna give me my needs; He knows them before I do. He's always going to be there. He's my covenant keeper."

Another pause.

"He gave me something no one else could ever give me—LIFE!"

Another pause. Another moment of letting go.

"My friends can make me happy one day and piss me off the next. With Him, I may have similar frustration, but the frustration is because I don't always understand or agree with His movements or methods. Yet I know He will always have my back. He will always fight my battles. Everything I step to, He's with me. I'm rockin' with Him 'til I go home. 'Til I can finally say I can put a face to the voice because I can see Him. I can see Him in my life. So, I keep cultivating this relationship. I want to be like Enoch where He just takes me. *Do you hear me Lord? Don't let me taste death if I don't have to.*"

She paused again to laugh at her own joke. She chuckled from a place deep within. A place that can only represent joy. A place that has seen no sorrow. Just as the Proverbial Woman, **she laughs at the days to come**.

"Father, just take me, but just make sure my children are grown so they won't lose it." She laughed again and said, "But just take me. I wanna walk that close to Him where folk say, 'What's wrong with her; she's so weird.' Yes, I want to be like David! I want to dance out my clothes for the Lord."

There was yet another pause, but in her pause, I could hear her smile. Her heart was smiling.

"It's dope! So, you know what? Maybe that's what my future looks like. Maybe that's the picture of my future. I want to be that woman that the world says, 'That's that chick that told me to have a relationship with Jesus.'

She sucked her teeth in a way that only a woman of a certain color can. It sounds like air escaping a tire and it's only made when they are thinking, *'you just don't know.'* Right after, she took a breath and said, "Yup, I want to have that welcome kiosk that introduces everybody to Jesus...that's what's up.

"There you go."

And with that she was done. I can always tell when she's done. When she says, "There you go," it's her ism and it means she's finished. However, I kept recording just in case something else was left.

"Well alright! Because we got it all!" I exclaimed.

She belted out a hearty laugh from a happy place. She chuckled because she reached the end. The recorder was still on, but I think we both knew. I knew with each tear and each chuckle she was finally letting go. I knew it was the end when she was grateful for being able to help so many of us by walking a road we had yet to walk. So often she guided us through and reminded us of our value. She made it through storms to help women like me navigate my storms. I love her and the space she's in and I'm excited at what's to come. So, I moved to close it.

I sealed the deal with, "We're finished!"

"It better be. I am all excited bouncing around in my seat. But I do want to wrap up this book with why and what this book means to me. I spoke this book to you, because I got tired of carrying around shit that wasn't mine. Ummm...shit that was way too heavy for me to carry. Shit that was stankin. I had flies following me like this was some real nonsense, what I was carrying. Shit that didn't fit, that didn't even resemble me.

"Now understand, there were times where I felt it served a purpose and it helped me get through some things. It was my fall back; it was a comfort I found in the discomfort of carrying that baggage. I leaned on it and it became my crutch. Like if you're on a bus and you're tired of standing so you lean on your bags, and then sit on your bags. And in the discomfort of that bag you're leaning or sitting on, you realize it gives you rest. So, at moments, dare I say, I found rest in my shit. But I got to a point where it's like God said to me, 'Where I'm taking you, that stuff can't come.' And I'm letting go, chick. And it..."

Her voice trailed off and the tears formed. Her voice began to crack, and she abruptly stopped. The emotion of that moment washed over her completely. It's the gravity of where she's been and the awareness of where she's going that suddenly became real. I was wrapped in the moment, and all I could do was share the emotion and be a witness to the breakthrough.

"I'm letting go and I'm grateful, I'm grateful, I'm grateful," she cried. "I'm grateful for that four-year-old that didn't fall and break. She held on to her secret and found the strength to endure and keep going. And I'm grateful for the twenty-year-old that didn't give up."

She exhaled. It was as if she was in a yoga class exhaling her 'letting go' breath, only she wasn't in a class; this was her life.

"I'm grateful for the woman that was married that didn't drive into that damn wall when she wanted to. I'm grateful that as much as I wasn't fully present for my children, I didn't totally screw them up—God willing." Another hearty chuckle followed that statement.

"I'm grateful that when I ran from that building, my fear that I would die as only a "nice person" never manifested because when God spared me, I decided that I would work to make a difference in someone's life. I'm grateful that I began to see that my storms weren't just for me and I was able to sit in those spaces and not lose it. Because if those storms were just for me, I promise you I would have. I had to believe that just as Jesus walked and endured to ensure we were saved, that I had to walk to ensure that the people placed in my life knew what it would look like to make it. They would know how to navigate these waters and have someone to talk to, to say I get it with no judgment. I had to show them that they didn't lose value. Jesus didn't lose value when they pierced Him or when they spit on him. He didn't lose value when they put the thorn of crowns on His head. And guess what? We don't lose value either. When life throws crap at us, we don't lose value; we increase in value. This book showed me my value increased.

"I don't care what anyone says, no one can take that from me because I have Him residing in me. That's what got me through these storms. So, I spoke this book because it's time to not forget but to let it go. I won't forget the four-year-old because she's a part of me. I won't forget the eighteen-year-old, the twenty-year-old, the forty-year-old. They are all a part of me but it's time to let them go. I don't need to lead with those things anymore. I love it. I'm excited to be in this space. I'm no longer defined by what happened to me but by whose I am."

Pause.

"Yea, I'm excited. I'm excited about what's to come. I'm excited that I can finally free my hands enough to receive things God has in store for me. My arms are open wide and I'm not afraid."

Her voice cracked.

"I'm not afraid anymore, chick. Now when I walk away from *them*, the only things they see are the wings that have grown in the place where there were once scars."

Then she busted out laughing through the tears and said, "Now you can say, you have actually seen a butterfly cry 'cause this butterfly is straight crying!"

At that, we both erupted in laughter.

"I don't have to hide my tears anymore, so I thank you for joining me on this journey. I thank you for enduring, and carrying, and weathering, all without any judgment. I love you, chick!"

And all that was left for me to say was, "Girl, I love you too! I love you to the moon and back and all around the sun. I thank you for trusting me to capture your voice on paper as you spoke this book. And you're right. Now I can say that I've seen a butterfly cry, and with that we can stop recording."

About the Author

Everyone has their inner battles, the ones that no one sees. I grew up in Bed Stuy, Brooklyn with a love for dance and music. They were my voice and helped me overcome insurmountable obstacles. From the age of four, I learned to be a warrior. My inner child is my engine, and her resilience continues to push me to levels I didn't think were possible.

During the time of the infamous 9-11 attack on the Twin Towers, I was once again called upon to rely on this resilience when I narrowly escaped the imploding buildings, and I was left to bear the weight of survivor's guilt. I vowed to help others and I rallied to summon my inner warrior as a pledge and a torchbearer. At my core I am a mother, a wife, a daughter, a sister, a friend, and a child of the Most High. As I embark on this journey of life, I humbly yet boldly wear the hats of author, life coach and podcast host for the *Let's Talk Relationship not Religion* podcast. I spend my days learning the art of dancing in the rain, finding the light within the tunnel, and embracing the fact that every storm isn't just for me. I invite you to connect with passion and not just with pitfalls, and above all celebrate your triumphs!

Please come connect with me: www.lisavtaittstevenson.org.

.

www.ingramcontent.com/pod-product-compliance
Lightning Source LLC
Chambersburg PA
CBHW050149110726
47898CB00008B/2731